JABARRI

BOOK 10

THE GIDEON BROTHERS

J. NELL

Jabarri

The Gideon Brothers

J. Nell

Published by SalteWorksWrites

Cover Design: M A Rehman & CFM Design

Interior Design: SalteWorksWrites

Editor: All That & Moore Editors

❀ Created with Vellum

DISCLAIMER

Disclaimer

This book contains material that is only suitable for mature audiences over the age of 18 years old. Strong language, violence, and explicit sexual content included. Please read the trigger warning before proceeding! Proceed at your own discretion.

TRIGGER WARNING

Trigger Warning!

This book contains sensitive material including: Sexual Assault, Rape, Violence, Suicidal Tendencies, Self-Harm, Vivid Nightmare Imagery, Childhood Trauma, PTSD, Torture, Childhood Sexual Assault.

CHAPTER 1

 kai

AFTER TONIGHT, everything is going to change, but this talk is so long overdue that it can't be put off any longer. I park my car in my favorite place, a little cut by the lake I discovered a while back after Alayna and I broke up. It's quiet and secluded, and I would come here and cry, scream, and just let out all of my emotions without the prying but caring eyes of my family.

It's crazy how one decision could cause a cascade of changes. Had I decided to go to a different college, my mother would not have been in that particular airport or run into Josh, and moved to Mississippi to run back into Josh. She would have never met Peter, or GrandPeter as I call him. Our life would be so different, and I would probably still be with Alayna. Instead, I went to college in Mississippi, and she met Josh and Peter, I am not with Alayna, but I am with him. If someone would have told me this was what was waiting for me when I went to college, I would have for sure called them crazy.

I am not into journaling, so my therapist suggested I video journal instead, and that has been working. I pull out my phone to start recording but I have to turn so the sun isn't drowning me out. *It's Friday, and tonight is the night we tell our family the truth.* I begin but pause because once I say the words out loud it'll be even more real than it already is. I tried to convince him to wait a little while longer, but he wasn't having it. My mom and DJ went to oversee moving my brother's and grandmother's graves closer to us. He was tired of my mom having to travel to visit her son. They requested a family dinner tonight, well my mom didn't. DJ did. He wants to make sure his wife has all the support she might need. So this nut says, let's just do it tonight since all the family will be there, and I had put it off for so long I couldn't deter him any longer.

I take the pause off, but a sound stops me, and I begin looking around. There is a loud popping sound that I recognize right away. Gunshots. I jump up and notice a group of men on the other side of the lake holding guns, and another is on the ground. My mind instantly puts it together, and I also realize that I just witnessed and possibly recorded a murder. *Fuck.* I think it's time to get my ass out of here, but I know as soon as I start the car, they will hear it. I can try to just stay here and just be quiet, yeah that's what… Something wizzes by my head before I can even make the decision and I realize they are shooting at me.

I run to the car as the bullets continue to race past me. I push start, throw in drive and haul ass. I take the narrow road so fast that if anything were to run out of the woods, it wouldn't stand a chance because I would not wrap myself around a tree trying to miss it.

I hit the paved road, cut right, and floor it. Hopefully with them being on the other side of the lake, I can get lost in traffic if I can make it to the highway. *Fuck!* The seclusion of the lake is what I liked about my spot, but now it may be an unknowing accessory to my murder. The highway is a long way away from here. That was one of the appeals of coming here, it is off the beaten path, and I can pretty much guarantee privacy, but today, there is nothing peaceful about being thirty minutes from civilization.

I look in the rearview but don't see anyone and breathe a sigh of relief, but that was premature when my back window explodes, and I know they've caught up to me. I pull my gun out, reach over my right shoulder, and fire back. I press the gas pedal like I can press it past the floorboard. It's early in the morning, I am miles away from civilization, and I am alone. It's time to call in reinforcements. My mom is unavailable, so there is only one other option.

"Hey, Kaitoa," I say, talking to the system Jabarri downloaded on my phone. "Call Him," I say as I concentrate on dodging bullets, and trying not to drive off the road.

"Hey, baby. You miss me?"

"Someone is trying to kill me!"

"What? Where are you?"

"My lake! Trying to get to the highway, but there are three cars coming for me, and I still have a ways to go before I can get there," I say calmly in the phone.

"Hold on," I hear him moving and then the roar of a car. "I've got your location. I'm close. Hold on, I'm on my way!" he says, and I wonder why in the world he is close to my location. He should be more than thirty minutes away from me. I push the thought out of my mind as I concentrate on driving and not running off the road or getting shot from behind. The phone chirps again, and I push the button on the steering wheel. "I called for more reinforcements, They are far away but on the way. How are you doing?"

"I'm going to be out of ammo, so I need to make something happen soon," I tell him. "Oh shit!" I scream and grip the steering wheel so hard my knuckles turn white, and that is saying something, considering my dark chocolate coloring.

"Skai! Skai," he screams through the speakers.

"Hold on," I say as the car rams me again. I pull my other gun out as the car hits my bumper causing me to spin out. I release the steering wheel, grab both guns, and shoot as the car continues to spin, hitting one of the drivers. His brain matter slides down the window, and I injure the passenger of one of the other cars. I drop the guns, grab the steering wheel, and gun it.

"I think I really pissed them off now," I tell him. "If you're coming you'd better hurry. They know I am not going to be an easy kill, so all bets are probably off now."

"I'm coming," he says as I tear down this back road, hoping for a miracle. More shots ring out, and I know I am going to run out of time and luck if something doesn't happen and fast.

"Shit! They shot my tire out, I'm literally riding on the rim. There is an abandoned industrial complex I have to take cover in here."

"Make sure you take your phone so I can track you," I hit the left, and the car almost flips but I barely keep it from happening. I stuff my phone in my bra, stop the car, and get out running. I haul ass, running as far away as I can to hide until help gets here. I make it to the last building, crawl through the opening on the side, and find a place to hide. It's so quiet, and I swear my breathing is happening in stereo. I will myself to calm down and strain to hear what's going on outside. There aren't that many buildings, so I know it is only a matter of time before they make it to where I am and I have no guns.

Uncle Atlas would be so disappointed in me. He has told me repeatedly to carry at least two extra clips per gun, and after the shootout at the compound, we have been being more cautious, but I didn't think I would need all that for an hour visit this morning.

They found me. I can hear them outside, and I grab a piece of wood to defend myself even though it won't do much against a bullet, and I brace myself. The sound of tires and yelling greets my ears, and I know he's found me. Gunshots ring out a few seconds before his car crashes through the garage door. Jumping up from my hiding spot, I run toward him but soon see the rest of the guys spilling inside to kill us both. He rolls the window down as I am running past the car and throws me a gun that I catch and begin shooting everyone who isn't him. He is next to me in seconds, and we make short work of killing everyone we can before more cars join the gun fight. As soon as they see my uncles coming, they scatter like roaches in the light.

He pulls me to his chest quickly, "Are you okay?" he breathes into my hair.

"I'm fine now," I reply, soaking up his love and strength before I push out of his arms just as my uncles enter the building.

"What the fuck happened?" Uncle Atlas asks, pulling me into a hug.

"Can we get out of here?" I ask.

"Sure,"

"Hold on, let's get pictures of these guys so I can run facial recognition," Jabarri says while taking pictures.

"Let's get out of here, your mom is going to have a stroke when she gets back," Uncle Seph says and I know he's right. *So much for the other talk*, I think as I get in the car with Uncle Atlas and head home.

CHAPTER 2

1 Year Ago
Jabarri

I loosen the tie pulling it off, opting to forgo wearing one tonight. Natalie's family is having a family dinner, and she asked me to please come so she doesn't stab herself to death at the dinner table. Their family dinners are nothing like ours,. We talk, laugh, plot, crack on each other, and occasionally get our asses whooped all in one night. Natalie's family is more strict and boring than a dinner in a cemetery. My brothers and I are close and are usually all up in each other's business but Natalie's parents expect to know each and everything that their children are up to. She is a few years younger than me, but her parents treat her and her brother like toddlers to the point of buying them their own house right next door to them. I think the only reason my biracial ass made it past the rigorous vetting session is my bank account. I got the feeling I was about several shades too dark for their liking, but the fact that my bank account had several more zeros than theirs was pretty much evening things out.

Natalie saved me in a way, I was dealing with a situation I was completely unfamiliar with and was going through women like tissue until I met her in a big box electronics store, getting ripped off by the salesperson. She was beautiful, with dark blonde hair, green eyes, tall and slim. I walked over. "They're ripping you off. You'll get a better deal if you reach out to the manufacturer." I told her. "They are charging you twice as much as you can get it someplace else."

"The money is not the problem," she says.

"I never assumed it was, but just because it's not a problem doesn't mean you should be ripped off,"

"True," she says, turning to really look at me. "Why don't you explain to me over lunch." She offered, and the rest, as they say, is history. I spray on my cologne and head to her parents' house. That lunch we went to that afternoon had me reaching out to all the women I was seeing and telling them *it's over* by that evening. Over the years, I have watched my brothers fall one by one for their wives and be happier than ever. At first, I wanted nothing to do with it, but the older I got, the more I desired what they had. Who I thought I wanted was not an option, so I gave up the dream until I met Natalie, but I guess nothing was going to be that easy.

I grab my keys and head out for a long night. I never prayed for or desired patience, but for some reason, God has been putting me in positions that force me to have it.

"So, Jabarri, I thought we would be planning a wedding by now," Amy, Natalie's mom, says as we are passing dishes of food and I have to refrain from letting my Gideon nature come out.

"We are moving at our own pace, Mrs. Rawlins," I reply with a forced smile.

"Mom, no," Natalie tells her.

"What?" she shrugs innocently.

"All your mother is saying is why should he buy the cow if he's getting the milk for free," Chris, her dad, says.

"Okay, I think I'm done for the night," Camryn, her brother, says as he pushes back from the table.

"Mom and Dad you both are way out of line. I am a grown woman and I will marry who I want to marry when I want to marry them. Thanks for dinner but I think Jabarri and I are leaving," Natalie says, dropping her napkin on her plate as she pushes back from the table.

"Wait, we didn't mean it like that! You guys don't have to leave,"

"No, we do, I can tell Jabarri is holding on by a thread to not be disrespectful, and honestly, I'm no longer hungry. Let's go," she says and I am in motion before she can get the last word out fully.

"Can we go get a burger, please," she asks once we get in the car, her head pressed against the headrest.

"Of course we can," I tell her, starting the car and pulling away from her parents' house. When I met, her I was running through women, I was actually jealous of my old ass brothers. All of them settled down with amazing women. I love my sisters. They are a riot, they keep my brothers on their toes and match them in every way. Aryan is the last man standing technically, but he is so in love with Brooklyn but is too stubborn to admit it. Hopefully, he'll be able to get the girl, leaving me the only single Gideon man. Natalie is beautiful, fun to be with, and easy to talk to. Things moved really fast after we met, but her parents were constantly in the middle of our relationship.

When I asked her why her parents were so involved with their kids' lives, she replied that's how her dad's parents are with them even to this day. It's extremely weird to me, seeing as how my parents are the exact opposite. They only get involved if we ask them to.

"We're having a family dinner."

"Jabarri," she warns.

"It's just dinner,"

"I know, but you know how I feel about that and why."

"Fine," I say through clenched teeth. When she originally gave me her reasoning, I agreed but now it bothers the hell out of me.

"Jabarri, we talked about this,"

"My family wouldn't care about it, Natalie, and they wouldn't say anything either," I told her again.

"I am not ready," I shift gears and hurry to get her food so I can head home. Some things need to change…soon.

"I know you are angry, and I am sorry,"

"I'm not angry."

If I were her, I would have been moved away from my parents, but for some reason, she and Camryn have chosen to stay under their parents.

"Please, I know you well enough to be able to tell when you are angry, Jabarri. I don't like making you angry, I will think more about it okay. Don't be mad, I love you," she says, covering my hand with hers on the gear shift.

"I love you, too," I flip my hand over to grasp hers and give it a gentle squeeze. She can always talk me off the ledge effortlessly. We talk about dinner, laughing at her parents' antics until we get to the restaurant. However, I do not feel like seeing her parents peeking out of the window with watchful eyes.

"Are you coming in?" she asks me when I pull into her driveway.

"Naw, not tonight. We have a lot to do tomorrow, so I better be getting home,"

"Jabarri,"

"I'm just tired, Nat, that's all."

"Ok," she says, obviously not believing me, and I don't blame her. I think I have experienced every emotion tonight but I really am tired at this point.

Getting out of the car I walk around to help her out of the car and walk her to her door. Pulling her into my arms for a hug, I kiss her on the forehead and wait for her to go into the house safely before I head back to my car.

I take the scenic route home. I am tired, but I am in no hurry to get back home. Before I realize what I am doing, I am sitting in front of her house. I have been worried about her, but I know it's not my place to check in on her, and I am sure she wouldn't want my help. I can remember the first time I saw her, tiny, beautiful, and mean as a damn rattlesnake, and I was halfway in love instantly. Then, her girlfriend walked in and shit went downstairs immediately. I acted an ass, she acted an ass, and I thought I was reading her wrong that she wasn't attracted to me, but when she melted into me at Peter's wedding, I knew it wasn't one-sided. But Joseph called me out on my shit, and I knew then I had to pull back before I made things worse.

I made peace with it for the first time in my life, not getting what I wanted. I tried to be somewhat cordial to her. I started dating a lot until I met Natalie, and just like the bitch that she is, the universe saw fit to have her and her girlfriend break up. So now I'm the one in a relationship, and she's single. When we got the call to come to the house because something was wrong with her, I had never in my life been so terrified before. When I saw her broken, hurt, and devastated. I wanted to go on a killing spree but ripping her house back to the studs helped. I wanted to be there for her to help her through this, but I kept my distance, and here I am sitting outside of her house like a stalker. *I shouldn't be here,* I think, before I put the car in drive and head home before I do something I won't regret.

CHAPTER 3

*J*abarri

"What's for dinner?" I ask our resident chef.

"Like it matters, we both know you are going to eat whatever I make," Jaasiel responds.

"I swear, since you got married, your mouth has gotten smarter," I tell him, frowning at him.

"Have you met my wife? She brings out the best in me," he says as he pulls out his pasta machine and I realize it's going to be a pasta night. I look at the ingredients on the counter and I figure out what he is cooking.

"I have indeed met your wife, and like I have told you several times before, you're lucky I didn't see her first," I say, grinning at him and he rolls his eyes at my words.

"You're not man enough for Parker, hell I'm barely man enough for her," he says and we both laugh at his words.

"Fettuccine alfredo? Isn't that Skai's favorite meal?"

"I am not even going to ask how you know that," he replies side eyeing me as he kneads his pasta dough. "But yes, it is alfredo and yes it is her favorite meal. I shouldn't be telling you this but Parker heard from Brooklyn that Skai is really struggling with the breakup so I wanted to cheer her up," he says.

"Y'all have her so spoiled. Savvy and her brothers started it and all of you reinforce it," I say, acting like I am not bothered by the fact that she is not doing well.

"It's okay that we spoiled your ass though, huh. Mom and Dad started it, and we reinforced it, but that's cool, though, right,"

"That's different,"

"Oh really? Please tell me how?"

"Never mind," I say, not wanting to get into a debate I know I would lose cause there really is no difference, and from the smirk on his face I know he knows I don't have a leg to stand on.

"So, is Natalie coming?"

"No, I asked. She declined."

"Really? Again?"

"Yes, again. You know not everyone wants to be around people all the time."

"Mmm, so defensive. All I did was ask a question," he says, knowing good and damn well he is pushing my buttons on purpose. I open my mouth to retort, but the front door opens, and family begins pouring in, including Skai. It's been years since I first met her, and I still have the same reaction whenever I see her. Every. Single. Time.

"Watch your eyes," Jassiel says to me as Savvy and Josh walk in the room. Swinging my eyes back to him, I narrow my eyes at him, and he throws both hands up. "I'm just trying to avoid having to dig a hole to bury your body in," he says. I roll my eyes at him before walking away. Truth be told he helped me out because I wasn't paying attention to anyone but her. She has lost weight, and she was already petite. When I manage to see her face, I can see the hurt still lingering in her eyes, and I want to hunt her girlfriend down and six foot her but I refrain… barely. We all have a seat at the table, and I marvel at how much our family has grown over the past several years. Besides all of the wives, Savvy kids, and their significant others, there is Peter and Lennox, T'Aundrea and Angie, Praise, Luke, Lucas, Liam, Eliza, and Emerson, not to mention all the kids that are running amuck around the house, and of course Sarai and Bubba who is damn near a teenager and acts like a freaking adult. Sarai is sitting in between Atlas and True, who is talking shit to her and she is the epitome of unbothered. Bubba reaches across the table and steals a shrimp off of her plate, and you would think the world has stopped spinning, "Uncle Daddy, he took a shrimp," she says, looking up at him, bottom lip trembling and a croc- odile tear hanging precariously off of her lash and I bite my lip to hold in the laughter, but I'm simultaneously impressed with her acting skills. Now, I wasn't expecting what came next, "It's okay, baby girl," he says, and Atlas, at his big age, picks up a piece of garlic bread and throws it at Bubba, who catches it midair before throwing it back and hitting Atlas in the forehead and we all burst out laughing at his shocked face. And if that wasn't bad enough, he grabs his butter knife, holding it up, and Bubba does the same, and they have a butter knife duel.

"Dear god, you've gotta be kidding me," Savvy says, looking at the crazy scene we are all witnessing. If the general scene alone wasn't surprising enough, seeing Bubba hold his own against Atlas was craziness.

"Okay, who's been training him," Atlas asks as he blocks another move.

"Me," Jaasiel says without pausing in his eating. Figures, the man who works with knives everyday could teach Bubba how to handle himself with them.

"Alright, cut it out," Josh says, and they both put their knives down. "And Atlas," he says. "You just got your ass handed to you by a freaking teenager."

"I demand a rematch," he tells Bubba.

"You're on!" Bubba replies, and Atlas gives Sarai all of his shrimp. Spoiled. I lean back in my seat and just look at my family. This, this is what a family dinner should look like. I look over to Skai, and although she is smiling and laughing, I can tell she is just going through the motions.

I also notice that Savvy has noticed, too. *Shit*, I think, yep, I am going to do something stupid. The clanking of a glass gets all of our attention and I focus back in on what's going on to see Shepp standing.

"Shepp?" Savvy says, looking at her son curiously.

"Um, well, in the past few years, I have had a lot of changes like running GP's hotel empire so I figured why not one more change? I've asked Isabella to marry me, and she's agreed," he's announces, and Savvy practically screams. She jumps up and rushes to her baby son, pulling him into a hug and then hugging Isabella.

"Why didn't you tell us? We would've helped you plan an ask party," Savvy says, pulling back. "Did you let anyone know you were planning on proposing?"

"I wanted it to be a private moment, Ma, and no I didn't tell anyone that I planned to propose. Once we are married, I also plan on legally adopting her daughter," he tells her.

"I can help you with that," Carla offers.

"Thanks, Aunt Carla," he tells her.

After Savvy finally releases him and Isabella, his brother comes over to congratulate him. I look over to Skai, and I catch her swiping a tear away before pushing back from the table to go congratulate her brother, too. Eventually, we all congratulate the couple, and before long our family dinner turns into a wedding planning session. Shepp and Isabella don't want to wait to get married so it looks like we're having another Gideon wedding soon. When no one else is paying attention, I slip away and head out front. As soon as the door closes behind me, I suck in the cool night air and release it as I take a seat on the front step of the house. I hear her before I see her, "Jabarri," her soft voice calls to me.

"What's wrong, Skai," I ask without looking at her.

"Can you take me home? Everyone is in there making wedding plans but I'm just ready to go home. I don't want to ruin my brother's celebration, but I am not in the mood to plan a wedding no matter how happy I am for my brother." she says, and I can hear the tears in her voice. I finally turn to look at her and I am answering before I can think better of it. I grab my keys out of my pocket as I stand, "Let's go." I tell her to head to my car and hold the door open for her. I slide behind the wheel and head toward her house. Her asking me for help lets me know she is desperate. I send a text to Jaasiel letting him know I am taking Skai home. She is quiet, looking out of the window, so I turn on the radio to fill the painful silence, and it might have been a mistake when Jason Mraz's *I Won't Give Up* begins to play. I reach over to change the song, "Don't," she implores and I pull my hand back to grip the steering wheel. I hear her sniffle, and I know she is crying. "That was supposed to be me and Alayna, planning our wedding. I don't know what I did wrong, why I wasn't enough for her. How could she cheat on me? In my house, in our bed? I gave her everything. I was loyal to her, I never lied, never cheated, my family became her family. I just don't understand what is wrong with me, why love keeps evading me," she says, breaking out in gut-wrenching sobs. I pull to the side of the road, put the car in park, unbuckle her seatbelt, pull her across the console into my arms, and just hold her.

"There isn't one thing wrong with you, Skai, nothing at all. Her cheating wasn't about you. It was about her,"

"Sure felt like it was about me. She did it in the most hurtful way possible," she says, but it comes out muffled from her face being buried in my chest. The first time I really get to hold her, and it's simply to comfort her, but I still feel like I won the lottery.

Before I can revel for too long she scrambles out of my lap, "I am so sorry, you are in a relationship and I don't want to be inappropriate with you. I'd never want to hurt Natalie like I was hurt. I really am sorry," she says, sitting back in her seat and buckling her seat belt.

"Skai, you don't have to apologize. I grabbed you."

"And I let you. You're in a relationship that wasn't cool. I will apologize to Natalie when I see her. Can you please take me home?" she practically begs. I put my seatbelt back on, put the car in drive, and pull away.

"Skai," I say, but she doesn't reply so I leave her alone and concentrate on getting her home.

CHAPTER 4

*J*abarri

It's been a couple weeks since our family dinner, and I can't get the drive out of my mind. When I got to her house, she was out of the car so fast I could barely get out of the car before she was in the house, yelling *'thank you'* as she closed the door.

"Jabarri! You're not paying any attention to me," Natalie says.

"I'm sorry, what did you say?"

"My parents are planning a party for the holiday,"

"Natalie,"

"I know, but if you could just make an appearance, I would really appreciate it,"

"Okay," I concede, "But it really will have to be a quick stop since Brooklyn is graduating, and my family is also doing something to celebrate her,"

"I understand. Are you still thinking about your family dinner?'

"Yeah," I replied.

"No, you're not thinking about taking Skai home," she says, and I look over to her. Natalie and I don't keep things from each other.

"She was hurt, it's very rare to see her broken like that. My brothers call her a walking menace. She is like a honey badger, cute to look at and mean as hell," I tell her and Natalie starts laughing.

"If I were you, I wouldn't tell her that,"

"Oh, she knows,"

"I really like Skai. I hate that she is still hurting, but please tell her she doesn't have to apologize to me,"

"I tried to. I was going to explain things to her, but she wouldn't let me. Honestly, it isn't for me to tell,"

"Of course it is! I may not want your whole family knowing, but Skai is obviously different," she says. I look over to her to see if she is serious, or not and she is.

"When are you…"

"I don't know, but I understand that I'm going to have to and probably sooner rather than later. You've allowed me to get comfortable, Jabarri, but I guess I'm going to have to blow my world up,"

"I would never leave you alone, Natalie. I'll help you with anything you need,"

"I know, and I love you for it," she says, leaning over to peck me on the lips.

Natalie

My parents have always been hands-on parents and that is putting it mildly. They have always been involved in every single aspect of both my and Camryn's life, school, friends, and especially significant others. Going so far as trying to pick girlfriends and boyfriends for us, but I swear their parents are the same way. I wouldn't be surprised if my parents told my brother and I that their parents were in the room with them, telling them how to fuck, what position, and even setting the mood for them. The only reason they haven't been around is because they took the ultimate world cruise, two hundred seventy-four days, eleven world wonders, and 60 plus countries but they are set to be home for this party. If I am going to get through the day, I will need Jabarri. Since I met him he has been saving my life and being an amazing friend and partner. We became close really quickly, he was so easy to talk to, and I found myself opening up to him about things I had never spoken out loud before, and I think I gave him the space to do the same.

His family seems amazing, but after we were together for a little while, I felt it was better not to get too close to them, even though there were more times than not I wanted to. They constantly reached out to me, inviting me to do things with them, but I always declined with some lame ass excuse until they got to the point where they just stopped asking. The family he has is the family I always wanted, I couldn't imagine our families meeting each other. My parents would be mortified. With as much money as the Gideons have, they are so down to earth and accepting of people, and even though my parents haven't stepped foot in a church in all my life, they like to act like they are good Christian people, more like hypocrites, but I wouldn't dare say that to their faces. Ugh, I don't want to sound ungrateful, I love my parents, and I guess they did their best, but a lot of their beliefs are ass backward. I want to go grab a gift for Jabarri because he deserves it, and gift-giving is one of my love languages, so I like to do it.

I drive to a new shopping center that's just about an hour away to go to the specialty electronics store. Luckily, I know exactly what I am coming in here to get for him. He was talking one night about the drive and monitor that was coming out that he wanted. So I went to work trying to find them, and I ran across this store, so here I am. I had the stuff ordered and shipped to the store, so it was a simple transaction, but on my way out of the mall, a dress catches my attention in a cute little boutique, so I slip in to see if they have it in my size. It's the perfect dress to wear for the party this weekend and I also want to see what else they may have that I can get for myself. This wasn't supposed to be a shopping spree, but why the hell not? I love to give gifts, especially to myself.

"Hi, what can I help you find," I hear the voice walking up behind me as I look through the rack to hopefully find my size in that dress.

"Yes, I'm hoping you have this dress in a… Yes, I got it!" I say, practically snatching the hanger off of the rack before spinning to the voice. "Do you have a fitting room…" I trail off when I see the person attached to the voice. *Shit*, I think this changes everything.

"Are you okay?"

"Um, yes, uh, can I try this on?"

"Sure, the fitting rooms are in the back," the smile has me hoping I am not the only one who is feeling this. Needless to say, I left with the dress, a few other gems, and more, Jabarri and I have to talk. I knew this would eventually happen, but I didn't think it would be like this and definitely not today.

This could change everything for Jabarri and me, and as much as my parents' overbearing nature has been a pain in my ass, I have never been without them, and honestly, I don't know if I can be. And as unfair as it might be, I would need Jabarri more than ever. Maybe I should have gotten close to his family after all, but then again, maybe not. I know they are accepting and all that but I don't think they would be accepting of this. I am sick to my stomach thinking about the possibility that my life as I know it now might be over. But it doesn't have to be. I can continue on as I have been, I think, as I put the bags in my car before sliding behind the driver's seat. But it's about time I be brave and live my truth. I put the car in drive just as my phone rings, "Hello,"

"How long do I need to stay?"

"Not long," I tell him. "But we need to talk,"

"Uh oh, no man likes to hear those words,"

"I don't think this will be a bad conversation. It's probably a conversation you've been wanting to have,"

"Um okay, but it might have to wait after the graduation and party. You know my family parties until the sun comes up,"

"Yes, I am aware. Whenever you are free is fine. What time will you get to the party?"

"It depends. If I leave there without making sure no one needs me to do anything I will be homeless," he says, making me laugh.

JABARRI

Of course, my family threw a hell of a party for Brooklyn, and we didn't go to bed until the sun was up. I spent a couple hours at Natalie's party, and I just about ripped all of my hair out. I don't know how Camryn and Natalie came from their parents; they are nothing alike. I started to come to the party in ripped jeans and a tee shirt, but I wore my signature black with my "hippie" hair down. That's what her grandparents called it the one other time I went around them, and it was down. I practically ran when Natalie said I could go, but now that I have partied, passed out, and then stuffed myself at breakfast. I am heading to Natalie's house to talk about whatever is bothering her. I have made this drive so often I can do without giving it any real thought allowing me to think about Skai at the party. She looked a hell of a lot better than the last time I saw her, but she went out of her way to avoid me, and I didn't push her. I pull into Natalie's driveway, and I didn't even realize I was so close.

I use the key, "Natalie!"

"Back here," she yells, and I walk towards the back of her house.

"I hope you're not back here trying to cook,"

"No, smart ass, I am not," she says with humor lacing her voice. I find her sitting at the kitchen table enjoying leftovers from last night's party.

"As 'traditional' as your parents are, I am still trying to figure out why your ass can't cook."

"I just never took to it. Now Camryn did, but my parents almost gave him a lobotomy, so he stopped cooking for them."

"Your parents are weird as hell."

"I never thought so. I always thought everyone's parents were like mine until I got older, and then I realized my parents are crazy as hell."

"Okay, so let's talk,"

"I met someone," she says, and time stops.

Three words. Three words changed everything. Three words I had been waiting to hear and finally Natalie said them. But with the revelation a new set of challenges presented themselves. Not for me, but for Natalie and I plan on being there to help her through this. But for the first time in almost a decade I am free to go after her, and I hope she's ready for me.

CHAPTER 5

*J*abarri

Even though for the first time ever, I am able to pursue Skai, but I have not made a single move. The last thing I want to do is make a move and ruin things before they ever get started. She is not an easy person, and she is not going to make anything easy on me, so coming to her half-assed is not an option at all, so I need to be strategic about things.

"I have a suggestion for you," Natalie says.

"What's the suggestion?"

"Just go to her and be yourself."

"Oh, is that all?"

"Yes, Jabarri, you are an amazing person. You are definitely not the same man you were when you first met. Let her see that,"

"You don't know her,"

"Maybe not, but I know you, and I know what you told me. Go to her and actually talk, no smart-ass comments or remarks, and go from there," she says before walking away.

I met her for lunch, but I wasn't much company since my mind was somewhere else. I watched her get into her car and pull away from the curb. I slowly make my way back to my car, thinking about the conversation I overheard about Skai, moving back to the house we remodeled and turning into herself. Savvy said if Skai continued to isolate herself, she was going to move her back to the pool house. I pull into the restaurant parking lot, park, and head inside; fifteen minutes later, I carry the bag with birria tacos, rice and beans, and chips and salsa. I make sure her food is good and head to her house. There is no telling how she is going to react to me showing up on her doorstep, but I have never been a coward, so I prepare for the fight I know she is going to give and head toward her.

Skai

I am so glad I always have my entire family's location and alerts set up to go off if they get within ten miles of my house. It gives me enough time to change clothes, get my hair together, and look presentable before they show up at my door.

I had to practically sign a contract in blood when I moved out, saying I would call someone if I was really struggling with my breakup. Here's the thing, I have been struggling, and even though I really loved Alayna and had long-term plans with her, I feel like I should've been past this, but instead, it continues to creep in at the most inopportune times and crush me with the weight. I gave her everything, shared everything, and she betrayed me in the most brutal way possible. Years down the drain, I can deal with it during the day but it's at night while I am in this house by myself or when I am at my mom's house surrounded by couples that I feel it acutely. DJ, aka Daddy Jag, made sure to completely remodel this house until it doesn't look remotely like the house Grand Peter gave me, but it doesn't mask the fact that she isn't here.

Brooklyn suggested I go to see a therapist, so I did, and I can admit that it helped some, but I know I have a long way to go. I peel myself off the couch and pad my way to the bathroom during the commercial break.

I look like hell, I think as I catch my reflection in the mirror, my hair is in an afro, I have on the same pajamas I have had on since Friday, and I have dark bags under my eyes. I can see the weight loss that I conceal from my family with layered clothing, but I can't really afford to lose many more pounds before I look truly emaciated. I gotta pull myself together; at this point, I'm just pathetic. I hear the doorbell as I am heading back to lay on the sofa and turn to see who popped up at my house unannounced.

"Jabarri!" I say, surprised and aware that he caught me looking just shy of a hobo. In lieu of a greeting, he holds up a bag from my favorite Mexican restaurant before brushing past and walking inside my house. The smell hits my nose, and my stomach decides to wake up and growl letting me know she's hungry, and I reluctantly follow him to my kitchen. I stand in the doorway and watch him bustle about my kitchen, putting my food on a plate and grabbing water, silverware, and napkins before pulling the chair out and looking up at me expectantly. I open my mouth to protest, but my stomach uses that moment to growl louder than before. I can't really remember the last time I actually ate, so I closed my mouth, crossed the room, and took a seat in the proffered chair. He sits next to me, and the silence is so loud it's deafening, but one bite into the taco, and I couldn't care less. I eat all of the tacos and rice and beans while he sits there snacking on the chips and dip.

"How long has it been since you've eaten?"

"I'm not starving, Jabarri,"

"You look like the skeleton from a high school science class, Skai," he says, and my decent mood is immediately gone.

"Is that why you came over here to see how bad I look, to rub in my face how stupid I was?"

"No, I..."

"Just leave. I'll transfer the cost of the food," I tell him, scraping the chair across the floor as I prepare to get up and walk him to the door, but the hand on mine stops me. I snatch my hand away from him as I glare at him.

"Can we not do this? I just wanted to come by and make sure you were okay. But come on, Skai, you have lost a substantial amount of weight. I'm just concerned, we all are. Don't make me leave,"

This is new. I know how to handle smart-ass Jabarri, arrogant

Jabarri, and even taken Jabarri, but a sincere Jabarri? That's uncharted territory, which is probably why I don't leave the table.

"I appreciate the food and you checking on me, but I am fine. I go to work every day and see my therapist; I am at every family function. What more do you want from me?"

"To be happy again. The light you used to have in your eyes is gone. The fire is no longer there. How can I help you get it back?" He cradles my face in his hand, and before I can think better of it, I lean into it.

"How, Jabarri?" I whispered in the quiet room.

"Like this," he leans over and kisses me really kisses me. His lips are soft and warm, and they have me melting in my seat until I remember he is a taken man! I pulled back from the kiss so fast I almost fell over backward in the chair.

"GET OUT," I growl at him.

"Skai,"

"No! There is nothing you can say to me. You are in a relationship, but you're over here kissing on me. I will not do to Natalie the same thing that was done to me. I saw my dad completely dog, disrespect, and cheat on my mom my whole life until she left him, and I refuse to do that to someone else. I want you to leave my house," I tell him before getting up and walking out of the kitchen. I wasn't in the best of moods before he came, and I feel even worse now. How could I do that to another woman? I sit on my bed until I hear my front door close, before breaking down.

Jabarri

How could I fuck this up so badly? But I had waited years for that kiss. However, her and I needed to have a conversation first. Now, I don't know if I will ever get the chance to talk to her and make this right. One thing for sure, after that kiss, I am not willing to walk away I am just going to have to think outside of the box. I head home but decide to make a phone call.

"What do you want? True and I are trying out our new guns, and you are disturbing us," he says, and I hear gunfire in the background. These two are certifiable.

"Gummy, I need your help, and I need you to keep this between me and you," I tell him. I hear shuffling in between gunfire until it's completely quiet.

"What's going on?" he asks seriously.

"I need you to send food to Skai for dinner. I would send it myself, but I don't think she would take it from me,

"What did you do?"

"Fucked up, and I have to fix it, but she has lost a lot of weight, and I want to make sure she has food to eat tonight even if she doesn't eat it,"

"What are you talking about?" he asks, concerned over his "baby," so I run down my visit minus the kiss and getting kicked out.

"I'm going to have to go get my baby and have a niece uncle day."

"I don't think she's been hiding it from Savvy as well as she thinks she is,"

"Savvy is no dummy, and I have already ordered food to be delivered later."

"Thanks, Atlas,"

"You're welcome. Now let me get back to my wife and guns," he says, disconnecting the call. I make another call to my hail Mary and pray this crazy ass idea works.

CHAPTER 6

S kai

I don't know why I said yes, probably because I felt like I owed her an apology. I knowingly kissed her man, and I enjoyed it. I thought about that kiss all night, and with it, I was wracked with guilt. I don't do cheating or cheaters, and for me to become one does not sit well with me. So, when Natalie called me a couple of days later to meet her for lunch, I reluctantly said yes, so here I am, meeting her to give her an apology. Personally, I don't really care for the woman, she keeps herself isolated from Jabarri's family, and to a Gideon, family is everything, but honestly, it's none of my business. If he likes it, I love it.

I enter the restaurant and give my name to the hostess, following her as she shows me to my seat. Natalie is already seated at the table, and I have to admit she is a beautiful woman, I can see why Jabarri is attracted to her.

"Skai," she says when I'm close to the table.

"Natalie," I reply, taking a seat.

"I was a little surprised you actually came."

"So am I," I reply. The server comes over and hands me a menu.

"What can I do for you, Natalie? Why did you call me to meet you?"

"Jabarri..."

"I am sorry, Natalie, it wasn't my intention to cross any lines,"

"Skai, Skai," she says, breaking into my rambling apology. "It's okay,"

"Okay? Okay, that I kissed your boyfriend?"

"Yes," she answers, and my jaw drops to the table. The server comes back over and takes our order before walking off.

"Okay, do you want to explain now, please?" I ask, completely confused.

"Skai, I am gay. It is something I struggled with for years, not wanting to accept it and basically fighting against my nature. When I met Jabarri, I wanted desperately to just want to be with a man. I recognized he was a very attractive man, but I wasn't attracted to him. I sure as hell was going to try to be or die trying. I did a pretty good job until I couldn't keep coming up with excuses to keep him at bay. So, one night, I was going to just let it happen," she says, frowning, her face up like it was the worst-sounding idea ever. "It lasted all of thirty seconds, my panties didn't even come off before he was calling me out.

That was the night I said the quiet out loud to Jabarri and admitted that I might be a lesbian," she says with tears threatening to fall. I sat there flabbergasted because out of everything I was expecting, it wasn't that.

"I ENVY YOU SO MUCH, Skai, you are able to live your truth out loud. You don't have to hide who you are or who you want to love. And you have family who love and support you regardless. I wish I was bisexual, that would make it so much easier, but if I can't tolerate physical intimacy with a man as handsome as Jabarri, I don't stand a chance. My parents consider themselves traditional, they mapped out their kids' lives before we were even born. They try to control every aspect of our lives. Hell, they bought us both houses right next to theirs with their money. I know now it was just to be able to control us.

If I came out to them, I would be completely cut off, Skai, from everything I have ever known including my brother. The time I have spent with Jabarri has been the most freedom I have ever had. He has shown me how family should be, what I could have, but he has paid a price for his love. His loyalty to me has prevented him from going after the woman he wants to be with, but I hope now that will change."

"Why, what has changed, Natalie?" I ask, feeling slightly overwhelmed by everything she's told me.

"I've met someone and just the little bit of time I have been with her and talked to her has changed me to my core. I no longer want to live the life my parents carved out for me; I want to be happy since life is too short. And Jabarri has promised to be by my side while I navigate this new future as a friend, he will be all I have once I stop hiding. But having Scottlyn in my life has made me realize what Jabarri has been missing out on all this time. I love him too much to be selfish."

"He doesn't have to be the only person, Natalie. Why didn't you let his family in?"

"I felt it was unfair too for me to build relationships with them under false pretenses. I knew I wasn't going to be with Jabarri romantically, and I didn't want to lie to them or get their hopes up about me and Jabarri getting married, and I didn't want Jabarri to have to lie to them any more than he already was. So, I kept my distance. I didn't care if we lied to my family. Hell, I have been lying to them my whole life. Trust and believe, though, I wanted to come to the family events. He would tell me about the shenanigans, and they got up to, and most of the time, he'd have some video of it, too, and I would cry laughing and then immediately be sad that I wasn't there."

The waiter left our food a long time ago and I picked up my fork and started eating because I am at a loss for words, and I need a moment to process what she just dumped on the table between us.

However, soon the food was gone, and I could no longer hide. "So why are you telling me this?"

"I was hoping that under the circumstances, the woman that Jabarri desires to be with and I could be friends. I know I am a coward and weak, but I need his strength, and I can't imagine being without him."

"First of all, you are not a coward or weak; we all need to depend on someone sometimes, but I still don't know why you are telling me this."

"Yes, you do. When he told me he kissed you he was the happiest I have ever seen him the whole time I have known him," she tells me, and I just sit there.

"So, you think I am the woman he wants."

"You know you are," another voice answers from behind me. *I've been set up.* I think as Jabarri takes a seat between Natalie and me.

"I am going to take my leave. Skai, thanks for coming and listening, and I hope you and I can eventually become friends." She stands, and grabs her purse before kissing Jabarri on the cheek and walking out.

"Skai,"

"You ambushed me."

"You wouldn't see me or take my calls, what else was I supposed to do? And if I had told you what she told you, would you have believed me? Besides, it was her story to tell, not mine,"

"So, you had her bring me here and then ambush me for what?"

"Stop that, Skai. You are one of the most intelligent women I know, but so there aren't any misunderstandings I'll make it plain. I want to be with you, Skai, and I've wanted to for a long time. Will you give me, give us a chance?" he says, looking into my soul. I have to get out of here now! I grabbed my purse, pushed back from the table, and was on my feet in an instant, but as fast as I moved, Jabarri was faster.

"No, Skai, no more running," he says as his hand wraps around my wrist like a manacle. "We are going to talk, today."

"Jabarri, let go of my wrist," I grit out slowly between my clenched teeth, and he releases my wrist but threads his fingers through mine, keeping me rooted in place. He stands and throws some bills on the table before leading me out of the restaurant.

"You're place or mine?" he asks when we are standing outside of the restaurant.

"It is way too hot out here for this. Let my hand go so I can leave."

"Tell me you really don't want to talk to me, and I will leave you alone…today. I will never force you to do anything you don't want to do, even something as simple as talking to me. So, look at me and tell me you won't give us this opportunity to talk," he says, and I begin to shift my weight from one foot to the other in nervousness. His face softens as he looks down at me, cupping the back of my head. "Why are you so scared, Skai, you know me. I'd never do anything to hurt you. Will you let me go back to the house so we can talk? I will leave whenever you ask me to. Can we go talk?"

Ugh, I hate this side of him. I think because as much as I want to bolt, his sincerity has me saying, "Yes."

JABARRI

When we made it back to her house, we sat in the living room. I made sure to sit in the chair, and not on the sofa. I wanted her to feel safe, and I also wanted to put some distance between us because my hands itched to touch her. It was disconcerting to see tough-as-nails and smart mouth-ass Skai be nervous. Honestly, she hasn't been the same since her breakup. All I want is to see her fight and fire back, but she has to give me a chance to help her find it again and us.

"So, talk," she snaps, and I smile. Now that's the Skai I know.

"Are you going to fight this, Skai," I ask her with a smirk as I lean back in my chair.

"Fight what?" she asks, eyebrow raised in challenge.

"Okay, if that is how you want to act, I'll do what you're too afraid to admit,"

"Afraid! I am not afraid of anything but my momma!" she says, and

I laugh because I completely understand. I'm afraid of my momma, too.

"If that's true, then come over here and kiss me,"

"Kiss you!" she says indignantly like I asked her to lick a gas station bathroom floor.

"Get your little fine-ass up, come over here, and kiss me. You know there is nothing stopping you anymore, so what are you afraid of?"

"Men," I think is what she says but it's so low I can't be sure.

"What did you say?"

"Nothing, but I am not coming over there to kiss you just to prove a point to you. We're not kids, Jabarri,"

"Trust me, the things I want to do to you aren't childlike at all,"

"Excuse me? Jabarri..."

"I'm sorry, kinda." Skai looks at me. I tell her and wait for her to comply. "Come here, Nöku Ahi," I partially ask, mostly demanding and to my surprise and relief she stands and walks to me. When she is close, I stand and wait for her to walk into my arms, "I want a chance with you, Skai. Do you want that, too?"

"I'm scared, Jabarri,"

"I know, Noku Ahi, but I got you. I've been waiting a long time for this. I don't intend to mess it up. I promise to be gentle and patient with you if you promise me the same thing,"

"I don't know what is going on right now," she says before resting her forehead on my chest, hiding from me,"

"We are agreeing to be in a relationship,"

"I don't date men, Jabarri,"

"You aren't dating me, Skai. As of right now, we are in a full-on relationship. Full fucking stop."

"And our family and Natalie?" she asks, making me cuss internally because I forgot about both of those things instantly. "She needs you, and my mom and DJ are going to flip their lids about us being together."

"If it is still okay with you, I would still be her friend until she is ready to tell her family the truth, as far as our family is concerned, I will defer to whatever you want to do. My brothers already know how I feel about you so they definitely wouldn't be surprised."

"You know when Uncle Anson and Meghan revealed they were married for years, and no one knew I thought they were crazy, but now I understand why they did what they did. With no one knowing there was no pressure or outside influences, they were able to work on their relationship in relative peace."

"So, you want to keep us a secret?"

"For a while, yes."

"And Natalie?"

"I'm okay with you staying her friend; she'll need you. When my brother threw me under the bus and outed me to my mom, I was blessed that even though it wasn't what she was expecting, she embraced me, learning about me and even becoming an advocate for me. But apparently, Natalie doesn't have anyone but you. I wouldn't ask you to not be there for her, but hear me clearly, Jabarri if we are going to try this, there must be boundaries. There is no need for her to continue to come to family events like she's your woman anymore, and I'm not going to compete with a fake relationship,"

"I can do that, but keeping it a secret is a short-term thing. We aren't a dirty secret, and we communicate about everything. There will be no misunderstandings. If something bothers one of us, we talk that shit out, not let it simmer between us and fester until it's about to rip us apart. If it's not something we are comfortable with talking about verbally, we will text, video message, or write to each other in a journal or something. We both need to be patient with each other and understanding."

"Okay, but I really need you to be extra patient with me. I haven't liked or been in a relationship with a man since I was a young teenager, and I am not very comfortable with men, not even you, so I am asking, please be patient,"

"I got you, can I kiss you?" I ask, pulling her head back to look down at her.

"Plea…" she doesn't get the rest out before my lips are on hers. I force myself to slow down so I don't spook her, but her nails dig into my biceps before tunneling into my hair. Feeling the bite of her nails scraping my scalp as she grabs handfuls of it and tugs has me calling on all the willpower I have, and some borrowed, to stop myself from laying her down on this plush rug and fucking her until we are both exhausted and dehydrated. I pull back just in time, cradling her tighter in my arms. I've waited years for this, and it was worth it."

Skai

It has been several weeks since my and Jabarri's 'talk', and our relationship has two speeds, fast and slow, but somehow it works. Knowing him for years makes it kinda easy, but trying to navigate a relationship with him is a whole new territory for us both. We haven't been physical more than kissing, and he hasn't pushed me for more. I think he can sense that I am not ready for that. It is so different being with a man. There are days I love it and others I want to punch him in the throat. I walk into my house, throw keys on the counter, and head straight to the refrigerator., I swear I am always ravenous after my therapy appointments but this time I'm prepared. I pull out the ingredients for a ramen bowl when the doorbell rings, and I know it's Jabarri. He takes one look at me,

"What's wrong?"

"Nothing," I say but continue to decide to add, "Sometimes I just feel like going to therapy is a waste of time. I get why Brooklyn felt I might have needed to go, but I really don't feel like it's making a difference."

"Hmm," he says, walking over to the sink to wash his hands and taking over cooking, ushering me to a stool.

"What is that supposed to mean?"

"Nothing,"

"Jabarri!" I snap at him because I don't feel like playing these guessing games with him tonight.

"Why don't you be real in therapy? Maybe you'd feel differently."

"And how do you know I am not?"

"Because everyone I've talked to who went to therapy and talked real shit might have had complaints, but it was never it's not helping. It may have been they were tired of talking about something, or it's hard, and they don't want to face whatever they are dealing with, but never it's not working. We have been in this unconventional relationship for several weeks, and anything more than kissing damn near freaks you out.."

"So that's what this is really about! You just want to fuck, and I am moving too slow for you."

"Sometimes you are the smartest dumb person I know, you know that! I am not the same young man you first met, I'm not driven by my dick, and I'd rather have you wanting me, begging me to slide your tight pussy down on my dick, than have a woman going through the motions because she's been pressured into having sex. You are more to me than sex, Skai, a lot more, YOU ARE EVERYTHING to me. But I want you whole. I need you whole, I need you to want to be whole, baby. Go to therapy and open up, and once you do that and you still feel like it's not working, then I will support you not going, but first, give it a real shot, please."

"I'm sorry, Jabarri,"

"You don't have to apologize to me, Nöku Ahi. I want you to be comfortable around me, to be who you are, and feel what you feel. Like your mom is with my brother, like True is with Atlas, and Parker is with Jaasiel. Hell, like any of the wives are with their husbands. Now eat," he demands as he pushes the bowl over to me, and I do. We eat lunch together, we talk about the upcoming family events, and we have managed to keep what we are growing together a secret, which is not a small thing in this nosey-ass family, but we have taken great pains to do so we're just not ready to let them in, and we agreed to talk to my mom and DJ first.

"Jabarri, will you stay with me tonight?" I whisper.

"Are you sure?"

"I mean, I'm still not ready.."

"I know that. I just want to make sure you're okay with me being here with you all night."

"I," I begin and swallow against the lump in my throat. "I trust you," I tell him, as soon as the words are out I realize they are really true.

"I would love to stay with you. I gotta head home and grab some clothes and I'll be right back. Do you want me to grab you anything while I am out?"

"No, I don't think so," I tell him as he washes the dishes. One thing I can say is when he is around I don't have to lift a finger. Honestly, if I really want to give this a real shot I have to open up more, not just with him but in general. And he is right, it's time I face some things I have avoided for years now.

"I'll be back," he says, coming around the island and kissing me before leaving the house. I head to take a shower before he gets back and throw on a nightshirt since I don't plan on going back out, just as he comes back. We decided to watch some movies and order dinner in. I have gained a lot of my weight back since starting this unconventional relationship. Before I know it, I'm waking up in his arms as he carries me to my bedroom. He pulls the covers back before laying me down and getting in the bed with me. I forgot to close my closet door, and I hate sleeping with it open. I've been afraid of the closet people all my life, and you cannot convince me there isn't someone in there watching you from in between your clothes when you go to sleep at night.

"Can you close my closet, please?" I ask, feeling bad that he has to get out of bed. True to form, he doesn't complain before climbing out of bed to close the door to my closet, which is the size of a bedroom, so I am shocked when I hear,

"Skai, who's shirt is this?"

"What?"

"This big-ass shirt, Skai, who does it belong to?" he asks, and I wake up enough to realize that out of all the clothes in my closet he picked out the one shirt that isn't mine.

"Why," I ask instead of answering him, enjoying his ire.

"Do not play with me," he says finally tearing his eyes away from the huge shirt hanging in my closet to look at me.

"Oh, you think this is funny, I see that big-ass smile on your face,"

"I think it's cute."

"Cute, huh? You're about to get somebody's face on the side of a milk carton,"

"Damn, well, that's going to be tough,"

"And why is that? I will beat his ass."

"Mmmmm, I doubt it,"

"Yeah, I definitely need to know whose shirt this is, especially since you think he can beat me."

"The shirt belongs to Atlas,"

"Well damn," he says.

CHAPTER 7

*S*kai

"I think this is the most productive session we have had, Skai anything that prompted this breakthrough?" Dr. Hunter says.

"Um, yeah, I was talking to Jabarri, and he suggested that therapy isn't working for me because I am not opening up for it to work,"

"Jabarri? Wanna talk about him?"

"I, whoo, it's really complicated, and honestly, I have never really looked honestly at my relationship with him," I tell her.

"Would you like to?"

"Yes, but I think it might be better if he is here when I do because there is a lot to unpack, and it may be more productive for me and him for him to be here when I do,"

"We can certainly do a couples session. Do you want me to schedule one for you next appointment?"

"Yeah, I think so," I tell her nervously, wringing my hands.

"Do you want to contact him and find out when he'll be free?"

"No, I am sure he'll make time,"

"Okay, let's make it for Friday, which is just a few days away. Are you okay with that? We can push it out further if you need more time."

"No, I have been dragging my feet for years over this. It's time I confronted it."

"Skai, I do not want you pushing yourself. It can one hundred percent cause more harm than good if you are truly not ready to do this,"

"I'm ready," I reply with a bit more bravado than I actually feel but I am going to stick by my decision.

"Okay, then we are all set for the day and I am so pleased with today's progress. I will see you in a few days," she says as we wrap the appointment up.

I am nervous driving home, and I don't know why, Jabarri has been nothing but supportive, sometimes too much. He still shows up for Natalie since she still hasn't told her family the truth, and for our family's stuff and still makes time for me. He stays at the house at least four nights out of the week, and I am quickly getting used to him being there, and that is a dangerous thing. The garage door opens when I pull into the driveway, revealing his car, letting me know he is already here. I pull in, park, and head inside to find him asleep on the sofa. I take a second to look at him and wonder how I got here with him. I ran from this man since the first day I met him, and now he is here in my home, in my space. What a difference time makes.

"Are you just gonna stand there and continue to stare at me, you pervert?" he says, making me jump.

"That's not what I'm doing?" I snap at him. Swinging his legs over the sofa, he is on his feet in seconds.

"Skai, what's wrong?" he reaches for me, but I back up.

"Nothing," I tell him, turning on my heels and heading toward the kitchen.

"Skai,"

"Are you busy this Friday at three?"

His eyebrows knit together as he stares me down for a few long seconds before answering, "You want me to come to a therapy session with you?" he asks, allowing the other topic to drop.

"Yes, unless you're busy, then I can reschedule it," I say, pulling the ingredients out to make dinner.

"I'll be there," he says, washing his hands so he can help me cook dinner. Together, we make quick work of dinner and clean up before falling asleep during the movie we were supposed to be watching.

I swear these were the fastest few days ever. Before I could blink, it's Friday, and now I'm in the lobby, practically sweating through my shirt.

"It'll be fine. If you are not ready, that's fine; we have time. I'm not going anywhere," he says, grabbing my hands to stop me from wringing my hands to death.

"Okay," I whisper just as Dr. Hunter calls us in.

"Jabarri, very nice to meet you. Please have a seat. Skai made a lot of progress during our last session and she felt if she was going to keep having this forward progress she needed to deal with some things she has previously had a difficult time facing," she says once we are settled.

"Skai, this a no judgment and no pressure zone, I only want you to do as much as you are comfortable to do. Understood?"

"Yes,"

"Good, so let's get started. Skai, you talked in previous sessions about your childhood and how that has severely impacted your life going forward but you never discussed it. Are you ready to talk about it now?"

"Yes," I say so low I don't think anyone could hear it, and Jabarri is sitting right next to me. I clear my throat, "Yes." I say louder and more confidently than I feel.

"First, I want to say that from the moment that I started romantically liking people I have always been attracted to both women and men. When I was younger, I was a grandma's girl, I stayed with her all the time. She spoiled me, and I pretty much got my way all the time, so it was a no-brainer to be with her. When I had to go home with my mom I was always looking for ways to get back to my grandmother's house. She always had medical issues, so she never lived alone, she either lived with her sister or later she moved back into her family's home. As I got older, she began giving me some freedom, for instance, she would leave me home alone as she went to the store or one of her doctor's appointments. I was still too young for my mom to be left alone, but my grandmother felt I was responsible enough, so she would do it, and neither of us would let my mom know because we both knew my mom would flip her wig."

"One particular day, I was home, and my cousin showed up to the house. I knew him well, so I didn't think anything of it, but I wish I hadn't. That was the first day he touched me. I was so confused I didn't know what to think. I was at the age that I was liking people, and some of the things he did felt good to me, so I felt like it was my fault, that something was wrong with me. He exploited those conflicting feelings, telling me that if I liked it, then I wanted it; why else would I be enjoying it? He was a teenager of about fifteen or sixteen, and I was ten, I think," I pause when Jabarri pushes a wad of tissues in my hand, and I realize I am crying. "He began coming over more and more, and since he was there, my grandmother began leaving me alone with him more and more, thinking there was someone there with me so I was safe. Little did she know she was letting the fox into the hen house. I would wake up to him standing over me, jacking off and ejaculating on my face or cornering me in the bathroom when everyone was home. It wasn't until I overheard my grandmother and aunt talking about him moving in with them that I knew that, eventually, he was going to flat-out rape me. I remember going home and asking my mom about her being molested by her cousin when she was a child. My mom didn't have the best relationship with her mother when she was younger, and she worked hard for her and me to have a better relationship. She wanted me to be able to come to her to ask her anything or talk about anything, and for the first time, I was taking her up on that. When I asked her, she finished cooking, fed us, and got my brothers squared away before sitting down with me at the kitchen table to talk just about her and me.

She said she also felt conflicted because when he would touch her in certain places, it caused a pleasurable sensation in her body even while her mind was screaming this was wrong. She said she would get up at the crack of dawn, leave the house, and stay gone until her parents came back home, and she would be safe. I remember her flat-out asking me if someone was touching me, and I lied, but I think she knew the truth. Don't ask me why I kept going back over there, but honestly, I loved being over there when he wasn't there, but when I woke up to him on top of me, I knew I had to get out. I just flat-out stopped going over there, and that made my mom even more suspicious. Once I no longer went over there, he eventually stopped going altogether, and at one point, he was homeless. I think he began taking drugs, and then he just disappeared. But the damage was done. I was terrified of men. I tried a couple of times to have a boyfriend, but both times were a disaster, especially when I had a complete meltdown during my first time, so women became my safe space.

When I met Alayna, the attraction was instantaneous, and I thought I had found my person until I walked in on her having sex in our bed in my house," I finish wiping the tears.

"Can I hold your hand," Jabarri asks and takes my hand when I nod.

"I hated watching what my dad did to my mom. He thought we were too young, and then when we weren't, he felt like we should stay in a kid's place. But how can we when he would get out of my mother's bed, and then go pick up another woman and be at his family's event with the other woman? It was in our faces, all of our faces, and he did not attempt to hide it. Then, he would play on my mom's fears, insecurities, and desires. He proposed so much to my mother with a new ring each time she could have opened her own jewelry store. So, I grew to truly detest cheating like it's a visceral hate. When she left him, I think me and my brothers were happier than she was," I turn on the sofa to face Jabarri. "When I met you, you stirred feelings in me that I had never felt for a man before, ever, but I was in a happy relationship. I did not want to feel anything for you, but I couldn't stop it from happening, so it was easier to snap at you, be a bitch to you, so you would stay away from me. I would have never left Alayna, and I would have never even considered cheating so where did that leave me?"

"Acting like a spoiled bitch?" he says, and a startled laugh slips out.

"Yes," I say, nodding in honesty. "But I don't want to run Jabarri. I

41

don't want to deny myself what it has been craving. I love you, and I may stumble a few times and revert to my safety net, but I am asking for your patience but also your honesty. I need you to call me out on my bullshit. That is the only way I am going to confront my shit and get better."

"I love you too, Skai, from the first moment you came bouncing in my house. I told you before and I'll tell you again, I am not going anywhere," he kisses my forehead before we turn together to face Dr. Hunter.

"Wow," she says, dabbing her own eyes. "That's what I call a break-through," she says, making us chuckle a bit before we continue our session, but for me, it felt like I released the weight of the world off of my shoulders.

CHAPTER 8

*J*abarri

After our therapy session a couple of weeks ago, she has been a different person, lighter, happier, and more at ease, and I am loving it. When she talked about her cousin abusing her, I almost lost it, but I made a mental note to find his bitch ass. But her vulnerability broke me down,

"You are the first man that I had real feelings for. You shook me to my core every time I was around you. Even with the few guys I was attracted to, I had never had such a reaction or attraction to one like I had to you. I did everything in my power to stay away from you, to keep you at arm's length. It was easier to keep you irritated with me then than to face my feelings for you and my relationship with Alayna. I guess everything happens for a reason. Even though I don't like the way it happened, I am coming to the conclusion that it had to happen."

"Would you have ever faced this thing between us?"

"No, I was content where I was. Alayna was easy. She was safe, and I was comfortable. I didn't have to face my past or even attempt to heal from it. Honestly, I feel she was just what I needed at the time, she kept me from spiraling into a depression, or worse. I would have married her, made a life with her forever, and I think I would have been happy," she says, and I shake my head in agreement because if things had been different with Natalie, I probably would have done the same thing and I say as much to her.

"We both would have made it work with our perspective partners and probably been happy."

"And miserable all at the same time," she says, laying her head on my shoulder.

"Indeed," I tell her. I love that she is facing this shit finally and that even though her cousin tried to, he didn't break her in ways she couldn't heal from. howeverHowever, I just want to have a conversation with him. But, the trail goes cold shortly after Skai stopped going to her grandmother's house. I want to ask Savvy, but then I would have to explain how I know, and we aren't ready to out our relationship just yet. Plus, Natalie still hasn't found the courage to tell her parents that her new friend Scottlyn isn't a friend but a lover. This is all a tangled mess.

Skai called me today to ask me to come over for dinner tonight, so I am heading that way. I made sure to grab her some flowers, and her favorite dessert. I ring the bell with my elbow since my hands are full, and she opens the door, and I forget to breathe. This is the most feminine I have ever seen her outside of wedding attire. She is a legging, sweatpants, and jeans type of woman, and it makes sense, seeing as she is either recruiting football players or is literally out on the field. The short pink ruffled spaghetti strapped dress with pink heels makes her look like walking cotton candy, and I have a sweet tooth.

"You look stunning, baby," I kiss her lips before handing her the flowers.

"You don't look so bad yourself," she says, walking back into the house, her face buried in the bouquet. I stop short when I get to the kitchen. She has gone all out for tonight; there are candles and flowers everywhere, there is soft music playing in the background, and a chef is in her kitchen making us dinner.

"What's all this?" I ask, pulling out her seat after she hands one of the waitstaff that must have come with the chef the flowers.

"I wanted to do something special for you. To show my appreciation for all of your patience and understanding. I feel like things have been very one-sided between us, and I want to rectify it, not because we're keeping score but because you are worth it, and I haven't shown you that."

"Nöku Ahi, you don't have to do that."

"I know, but I wanted to," she says. She really is a different person now, and I love it, but I also don't want her to change so much she forgets the woman she was when we first met. I fell in love with her mean-ass. We talk about our day as the chef makes a mouthwatering meal before cleaning up and leaving us alone still talking.

I look over to her when she doesn't respond to me, and see that she has fallen asleep sitting up in the chair. I get up and turn all the lights off before coming back over to her, picking her up, and carrying her to bed. My hands shake as I pull off her shoes before peeling the dress away from her chocolate skin, leaving her in just her panties. She is always in her pajamas when I stay the night, so this is my first time seeing her body. She is pure perfection, small, tight, and compact. I finish taking the dress off and carry it to the closet to hang it up and grab a sleep shirt, but stop myself. I snatch Atlas' shirt off the hanger and replace it with my dress shirt, slide my t-shirt over my head, take off my shoes and pants, and put my pajama bottoms on. Walking back into the room, I take the t-shirt I just took off and pull it over her head, pushing her arms through the sleeves and pulling it down her body. I swear this girl sleeps like the dead. She didn't even flinch. I turn the lights off and turn on the TV because she has to sleep with it on or she will wake up. I found out the hard way. I climbed in bed, pulling her in my arms before immediately passing out.

SKAI

Well, last night did not go as planned. I wanted it to be our first time, but instead, I fell asleep at the kitchen table. Ridiculous. I guess it wasn't meant to be. I set the cruise control and settled in the car for the three-plus hour ride to Natchez to see about a tight end Saint wanted to recruit. I find a good station and concentrate on the road. I had to talk Jabarri out of coming with me on this trip. I had to remind him I had been doing this for a while now alone. He didn't like it, but he reluctantly went along with it, having a job to complete today helped, but he made sure my location sharing was on, and I had a backup gun for my backup gun.

And even though I train with my uncles regularly, he has insisted on him and I training, so we'll start that as soon as I get back home. The man is paranoid. *Andy Grammer* comes on, and it is a song I am not familiar with, but I love him, so I turn it up and immediately fall in love with the lyrics. As soon as I stop for some food, I send the song *Good In Me©.* I grab a breakfast sandwich and some apple juice and get back on the road.

It was a good visit, and I think I can convince him to come to Mississippi to play for Saint. I set up for him to come and visit the college with his parents, and I know Saint will seal the deal. The man has a silver tongue and can damn near convince anyone to do anything. I didn't get a hotel room, the plan was to drive back today, but I am more tired than I thought I would be. I grab my phone to find a nearby hotel, but before I can search for one, the phone is ringing.

"Jabarri," I say in lieu of a greeting.

"How did your visit go?"

"It went well. I'm pretty sure that once they visit Mississippi, they'll sign with Saint,"

"Good. Are you on your way back now?"

"Yeah," I say a little unsurely.

"Hmm, you don't sound like you are sure about that,"

"I am a little more tired than I thought I would be,"

"Mmm, well, can you do me a favor?"

"Umm, sure, what is it?"

"Go to this address," he says, and my phone chirps notifying me of a text message. I put the address in the GPS and head that way, it's not far from where I am. I stay on the phone with Jabarri, telling him about the young man and his stats.

"Wait, it's a hotel,"

"I know. Give them your name at the front desk and call me back when you reach the room."

"Okay," I say, curious about what he is up to. I give my name to the woman at the desk, show her my ID, and she hands me a key card. *The suite, of course.* I think when I get to the room. I open the door, walk into the living room, and see a clothing rack, bags, and flowers. There is a card in the flowers,

I've got something special up my sleeve for us tonight! I couldn't resist planning a little adventure just for you and me. Get ready for an evening filled with good vibes, laughter, and, of course, a dash of surprise.

I won't spill the tea on all the details, but picture this: a night where it's just us, soaking in each other's company and making memories.

So, throw on the outfit I chose for you because tonight is all about us. I can't wait to see that beautiful smile of yours as we dive into the fun I've got in store. Get excited – it's going to be a night to remember!

Looking forward to our adventure,

Jabarri

He's here? I look at the time he said for us to meet, and I rush into the bathroom to wash and change. He thought of everything; all I had to do was get dressed. I didn't even bother to look at the dress he bought. I take my shower, lotion myself down, put on the bra and panty set he picked out, do my makeup, and finally reveal the beautiful dress he picked out. The one-shoulder-tied neck dress fit me like a glove, I put on the heels on, grab my keys, and head out. I am giddy like a schoolgirl as I ride the elevator down to the lobby, but when the doors open, I lose my breath. Jabarri is standing there and he looks amazing in his suit standing in the lobby waiting for me. My face splits into the hugest smile I can manage, and I rush into the open arms waiting for me.

"What are you doing here? Where are we going?"

"So impatient, and I couldn't be away from you, not even overnight,"

"I was coming home tonight, Jabarri."

"Well, now you don't have to. Come on, let's go, baby," he takes my hand to walk me out and to his car opening the door for me. He gets in the driver's seat and takes off smoothly down the road. He parks and comes around to help me out,

"A dance studio?" I ask, but he doesn't answer just ushers me inside. And once again, I am at a loss for words. There is a table set up on the side of the dance floor, and the room is blanketed in flowers and candles. The table is gorgeous, and there are domes covering dinner plates. He helps me sit, and a server comes over out of thin air and begins to serve us. Music is playing in the background, as we eat the delicious meal. When we get to dessert, I understand why he chose here to have dinner.

"I listened to the song you sent me this morning,"

"What did you think?"

"It's beautiful. So I searched to find a song that embodied how I feel about you and came up with this," he says seconds before the lights dim and the most beautiful music begins playing. A couple appears on the dance floor and dances to the song, telling the story of us through dance.

As I watch, he pulls me out of the seat into his lap and he holds me as this couple glides across the floor. Between their interpretation of our story and the words to the song, I am a sobbing mess when they give their bow.

"Don't cry, Nŏku Ahi. I want you happy, not crying."

"They are not mutually exclusive, Jabarri. I can be happy and cry. You make me happy. This was," I take a deep breath because I can't think of adequate words to describe what he did tonight means. "This was everything. What is the name of the song?"

"*Turning Page©* by *Sleeping at Last.*"

"So beautiful,"

"I agree, will you walk down the aisle to me to this song?"

"Jabarri!"

"Are you proposing to me?"

"I am just asking you a question,"

"I'll answer it if and when you propose," I tell him. The song ends, and the couple leaves as quietly as they came.

"Hmm, fair enough. One more favor?"

"Mmm," I hum.

"Dance for me?"

"Dance for you?" I am shocked by the request, I haven't danced in front of anyone in years. I started out doing cheer dance when I was five, my mom put me in jazz, ballet, ballroom, contemporary, and hip hop. I was a majorette in college but stopped dancing once I graduated. That explains the dress. "Is there a song you want me to dance to?" I ask noticing we are completely alone.

"Whatever song you want to dance to me with," I hop out of his lap, take my shoes off, search my phone for the song, and begin stretching in preparation to dance for him. This is crazy. I am giving this man a private dance, Jabarri! What reality am I living in? I find the song I want, connect to the Bluetooth, and press play. *Jazmine Sullivan's On It* comes on, and I close my eyes and let the music move my body. I forgot how freeing dancing is for me, to just stop thinking and just feel the music take over. I glide across the floor, spin, fall to the floor, and do it all over again, moving however the music tells me. I finish on the floor, back arched, one foot pointed, the other knee bent, pulling my hair and breathing hard. Before I can catch my breath, he is on top of me, kissing the little bit of breath I have away.

I widen my legs to make room for him as he plunders my mouth, coaxing moan after moan out of me. I pull the tie binding his hair, and it falls like a silken cloth shielding us from outside view. I grab it and hold on for dear life, and his hands travel my body, touching everywhere.

"Do you know how beautiful you looked dancing? How sexy? Do you know how bad I want to explore your body from the inside out? Lick every inch, fuck every hole? Do you know how bad I just want you?" he says between kisses, and my body and mind are in a heated battle. I want him, but I am scared to have a repeat of the first time I was with a man. But I am older now, and this isn't a teenage boy who barely knew what he was doing; this is Jabarri, my Jabarri. "But we aren't ready, and I can wait. Besides, our first time is not going to be on the floor of a dance studio. Wrap your arms and legs around me," he demands, and he stands with me in his arms like I weigh nothing. He sits me in my chair, kneels in front of me, and puts my shoes back on. I am not sure why, because he carries me out of the building back to his car.

JABARRI

We left for home early the next morning. Skai led, and I followed. I don't know how much longer we can keep whatever this is hidden. I want to say we are in a relationship, but I can't until the situation with Natalie is squared away and she doesn't seem to want to tell her parents anything anymore. I think she is enjoying having her cake and eating it, too. She's gotten to the point where she is lying to her parents, telling them she is with me when she is really with Scottlyn. She's had me put her security camera on her back door on a loop so she can sneak in and out of her house without her parents knowing. Generally, I wouldn't care, but until she settles this with her parents, my and Skai's relationship is on hold. But truthfully, even if she told her parents today and blew up her life Skai and I have to tackle our family. I don't know how Josh or Savvy will feel about her and me being in a relationship. This really is a cluster fuck of a situation. What would I do if they were against our relationship? Would I sacrifice my family for her? Without question, I don't want to have to make that decision for me or her. She stirs in my arms, and I know she is waking up.

Her therapy is going better, her heart is healing, and she is accepting that the things that were done to her weren't her fault. Truthfully, the things people chose to do to her have nothing to do with her and everything to do with them. But her mouth, that shit, is still razor sharp. I called her a tiny big mouth and she called me Barbie, her new nickname for me. Out of all the damn nicknames she could have come up with from Jabarri, she settles on Barbie. But honestly that was the first time I saw the old Skai peeking back through the shell of the woman that has been walking around since Alayna betrayed her.

"Did you drool on me?" I ask her when she lifts her face off of my chest and wipes her mouth.

"No, I didn't drool on you! You get on my nerves, I was touching my face because I lost feeling in it after laying on your Nestle Crunch-covered chest," she says, and I burst out laughing.

"Now you know you capping. My chest is smooth as a baby ass,"

"Yeah, a baby porcupine,"

"Oh, I see someone woke up with a smart-ass mouth this morning,"

"I wake up smart every morning," she says, climbing out of bed and damn near running to the bathroom. She uses it, washes her hands, stands in the doorway of the bathroom, and opens her mouth to say something when the doorbell rings.

"The notification didn't go off," she says, rushing over to her phone to check and remembering both of us putting on phones on silent so we could get some sleep. She checks the camera and cusses, making me look and see Alayna standing on the doorstep. "What the fuck! Let me go tell her to get her ass back to wherever she's been."

"Don't do that. Go see what she has to say. This may be your chance to get some answers. I'll stay in the bedroom out of sight. If she ain't saying nothing you want to hear, tell her ass to leave," I tell her, and she nibbles on her lip before saying okay and heading to the front door.

SKAI

I open the door, bracing myself for the feelings to come rushing back, but it never happens.

"You got some fucking nerves."

"I was hoping enough time has passed so we can talk."

"Girl, the only reason you're not waking up dead right now is because I am trying to be a better me. Come in. Let's get this over with so you can go back to wherever you've been, and I never have to see you again,"

"Wow, the house looks nothing like it did,"

"I removed every trace of you, but I know you didn't come here to talk about decorating,"

"I have had a lot of time to think about what I did, and I think I wanted you to find out. I wanted you to feel the same hurt you inflicted on me,"

"Hurt? Alayna, what the hell are you talking about?"

"You know exactly what I am talking about! You cheated first!"

"With who?"

"Jabarri!"

"Never. Not once,"

"You might not have cheated physically, but you did emotionally, Skai,"

"Are you slow? Is this you taking responsibility for your actions?"

"How can you not see it? I saw the attraction he had for you, hell, everyone did, and you refused to stop being around him!"

"No, I refused to stop being around my family, Alayna. Jabarri is my stepdad's brother. My mom lives in a house with her husband and all of his brothers. The only way I could stop being around him would have been to stop being around my family. I can't stop someone from being attracted to me, but what I can control is me, and I have never fed into or encouraged what Jabarri may or may not have felt for me. I loved you.

I was faithful to you! I would have never cheated, I would have never done you like my dad treated my mom, ever! And I would have never left you."

"Why couldn't your family have its own time together so they didn't have to be involved?"

"So let me get this straight, my family needed to have separate family time because you were insecure and didn't want me to be around Jabarri? Funny how you talk about his attraction to me being the issue, but I can recall you joking about one of the professors at my job liking me. You didn't have a problem with me going to work every day. You didn't expect me to leave my job or for my job to change my schedule so I wouldn't cross paths with him. So it's not about that. It was simply about Jabarri," I tell her.

"You're damn right it was."

"But why?"

"Because you were different with him. That's how I know you were cheating with him,"

"You're ass is delusional, you know that? I'm going to tell you right now, outside of me detesting cheaters, the reason I can prove I didn't cheat is the absolute fact that he wouldn't share me with anyone,"

"It doesn't matter. You're not going to own up to what you were doing behind my back,"

"Oh, like you're doing?"

"You're a fucking bitch! A black heartless bitch! You are all I had, and you fucked me over for a man! And he will never be with you!"

"You're going to watch calling her out of her name," Jabarri says from the doorway, and her eyes bug out of her head at him standing there, obviously fresh out of bed.

"I knew it! Are you going to stand there and still lie?! You were just waiting to have a reason to kick me to the curb so you could spread your legs for him! You're a fucking lying ass whore!"

"I know one thing, that's the last time you are going to call her out of her name,"

"Fuck you, bitch,"

"Now wait a damn minute, I let you slide fucking a bitch in my bed, and I still let you slide calling me out of my name just now but talking reckless to him is going to get you fuck up expeditiously,"

"You're taking up for him! You sacrificed me, didn't blink throwing me out on the curb, but will stand there and defend him!?"

"Man, I've had enough of this. Get the fuck out," Jabarri says, and she springs up from the seat, so mad the tips of her ears are tomato red.

"This ain't your house! You can't put me out,"

"I just did!" he says and the next events happened in slow motion and fast forward simultaneously. She turns to him, hocks up phlegm, and spits on him before turning around to me. I punch her so hard that she flies back on the sofa blood sprays everywhere, and I am on her before the second bounce. I punch her again and again before choking her and slamming her head on the back of the sofa. She claws my face, drawing blood, causing me to loosen my grip on her, allowing her to push me off of her. I stumble back, and she hops off the sofa and punches me in my temple. I jab her in the eye, the skin underneath it splits open and her eye instantly swells. I draw back and crack her jaw, before hitting her dead in the mouth, causing both lips to burst open. I pick her ass up and slam her on the coffee table, breaking it before I kick her so hard she slides across the floor. Before I can do any more damage I am lifted off of the ground and set behind Jabarri.

"I suggest you leave before I let her go," she spits on the floor, and in the midst of blood and spit are a couple of teeth. She struggles to stands, holding her side. I'm sure I broke a few of her ribs when I kicked her.

"You should probably go to the hospital and have your side looked at," he tells her. His arms band around me, holding me back, when I come from behind him and stand to his side. I look at the woman I loved for years, the woman I planned to spend the rest of my life with and feel nothing but empty regret. The tears in her eyes when she looks at me soften me a little, but I am done nonetheless. I watch her leave, dropping to the sofa when the door closes, and hiss in pain when Jabarri presses a cloth to my face.

"Your face, baby,"

"It'll be fine," I tell him, holding the cloth.

"Are you okay," he asks and I don't have an answer for him. My face hurts, and where she hit me hurts but hearing how she thought about me might hurt worse.

"I failed her," I tell him.

"No, she failed you and your relationship. She should have come to you with how she felt instead of acting in retaliation for her preconceived notion that you were unfaithful."

"I have never felt for another man what I feel for you, and it scared me when we first met, but no matter how much I denied it, she still saw it. I was supposed to be a safe place for her, and she was supposed to be a safe place for me, and I let her down, Jabarri. Yeah, she should have come to me, but she was here in Mississippi because of me, around my family, I should have done better."

"Don't do that, don't take all the blame. Even if you insist on taking the blame, it's not all on you. She has a lot of the blame on her shoulders, too. It's all about communication, and she didn't give you that. Come back to bed so I can tend to you. I want to hold you," he says, and I am too tired to argue, so I let him pull me back in the bedroom into bed, and even though I just got up a little while ago, I fall asleep almost instantly.

SKAI

Lennox is retiring, and we have decided to do a Gideon version of Lip Sync Battle, Lennox's favorite TV show. I need to get to the house to rehearse our songs and performance. I grab an extra set of clothes to change into for afterward since we're supposed to go out to dinner. I shove the clothes in my bag and brush past Jabarri without saying a word to grab my shoes and other stuff.

"Skai, are you gonna keep giving me the silent treatment?" he asks as he watches me move around my bedroom.

"I don't have anything else to say, Barbie." I call him the nickname I gave him.

"Please, Skai, just listen to me."

"For what, Jabarri? I told you how I felt, and you told me I was the one being unreasonable. She called you and you got up out of my bed with me to rush to her! And if that was a one-time thing, I may have let it slide, but over these past several weeks, it has become a common occurrence,"

"I am only gone for less than an hour in most cases,"

"I don't give a damn if you were gone for less than one minute! You getting up out of my bed in the middle of the night to run to the aid of another woman is not going to fly with me. I know she is your friend, and you promised to be there for her, and I am okay with that, but what I am not okay with is her constant and increasing need for you. She was supposed to be telling her parents that she is gay, but instead, she is using you to front for her parents and enjoying her relationship with Scottlyn. She has her family believing that Scottlyn is a friend! Even so, what butters my biscuits is the fact that she constantly has you putting us at risk with her requests of you, and it's pissing me off that you keep going for it. That you expect me to just eat it!"

"You're making a mountain out of a mole hill, Skai, you knew the situation from jump, and now you're frustrated that it's inconvenient? You are being ridiculous being jealous of a woman who isn't attracted to me at all, and I'm not attracted to her,"

"Are you still planning to take her to the retirement party?"

"I was,"

"Why, Jabarri?"

"She's meeting up with Scottlyn later, and it's not like we can go together,"

"Okay, so you'd be okay with me going with a man?"

"Why would I be okay with something like that?"

"Exactly! And you only say that because you know I would never date any other man than you! Okay, well, then what if I showed up with another woman?"

"Our little secret situationship wouldn't be a secret anymore,"

"Sometimes I swear you are not a real Gideon, but then again, you were conceived from one of your mother's older eggs! None of your brothers would dare expect any of the women in their lives to accept what you think I should. But don't worry about it, I'll make it easy. You won't have to worry about me being *'jealous,'* " I say with air quotes. "Don't come back here until you can get this shit straight with Natalie. I would never expect you to accept what you think I should, and that is why I am going to take myself out of the equation altogether," I tell him as I angrily zip my bag and storm past him and out of my house. I get in the car and leave the driveway so fast there is actual smoke coming from my tires. Halfway there, I begin to feel guilty for trying to force him to choose between Natalie and me. I know she needs him, and it's not a matter of being jealous it's about respect and the lack of it on both of their parts. I make it to my mom's in record time, we run through the routine, change, and head to dinner. The entire time I am running off of pure anger, but I put on a front so no one gets to asking me any questions. Luckily for me, since the breakup, no one pushes me too much so I make it through the night without any problems. But once I make it back to my house, and he isn't there, the loneliness hits me hard. The party isn't for a couple of nights, tomorrow when I get to work, I am going to ask Saint to send me someplace far away so I won't be here until it's time for the party. I shower again and don't bother with pajamas as I crawl into bed and into a fitful sleep.

"Saint!" I yell for my brother across the field the next morning when I see him getting ready to go towards the other goal post.

"What you want, big head!"

"First of all, I am the best-looking one of our mother's kids,"

"Please, you see all this six-plus feet of pure dark chocolate perfection?"

"Don't make me throw up," I say as I pantomime, throwing up.

"What do you want, sis?" he asks, laughing at me.

"Isn't there a recruit you wanted that was in Seattle?"

"Yeah?" he asks curiously because when he first mentioned it, I absolutely refused to go all the way over there.

"I'll go," I tell him, and he just looks at me for a long while before saying,

"Okay, Skai, set it up,"

"Thanks, Saint," I say seconds before he pulls me to him in a hug.

I head up to my office to make travel arrangements. I turn on the wax melter and some music as I book my flight, a rental, and my hotel. I pull out my phone and dial,

"What you want, shorty,"

"Shut up. I was taller than you for years!"

"Over twenty years ago. What do you need, sis?"

"I need a hotel in Seattle for a few nights,"

"I got you," he says, and I hear him clacking away on his keyboard in the background. He has done so well running Peter's business that Peter has pretty much stepped away from the business completely.

"Okay, I have you booked at the Royale penthouse suite. It's right on the water. You'll love it. When you get there call the number I text you, and Nathaniel will pick you up."

"I was renting a car. You know I like to be able to be on the go,"

"Mush," he says, calling me his childhood nickname. "It is a hotel car, guests can use the cars. No need to spend money on a car."

"Oh, okay. Is that one of your ideas, or did Peter already have that set up?"

"Naw, that was all me. It's a five-star hotel, guests are spending a grand a night minimum. The last thing we can offer is a complementary car for them,"

"I bet your hotel stays booked."

"It does, but there is an owner's penthouse, and that is where you'll be staying,"

"Thanks, Shepp."

"You're welcome, sis," he says, and I hang up. So the only thing I need to book is my flight. I open the search engine, type in Continental Airlines, and book to leave early tomorrow morning. I would have left today, but I haven't packed or called this kid and his parents. I secure my ticket, and call the Colfax's. They were excited to hear from me, and I made an appointment to meet with them the day after tomorrow. A knock on my door startles me a bit. "Elias," I say, grabbing my chest to try to slow my heart back down.

"You got a moment, Coach?" some of the faculty has taken to calling me coach because I work with the players and also because you can find her or me out on the sidelines with Saint at any given time.

"Sure, what's up," I ask, thinking again what a nice-looking guy he is. He is one of our physics professors, a little over six feet with a runner's body, green eyes, and dark blond- light brown hair, and the glasses make him look like a sexy nerd. The man is, in one word, adorable.

"Well, this is a little embarrassing and a bit unorthodox," he says, looking nervous and peaking my curiosity. I get up and close my office door before retaking my seat.

"Whatever you say here stays here. What's wrong?"

"Praise," he simply says. I look at him, waiting for more before it clicks.

"My cousin?" I ask, thinking of the woman Uncle Joseph and Aunt Joyce unofficially adopted.

"Yeah, um, is she seeing anyone?" he asks, and I blush for Praise.

"Nope, not as far as I know. She's too busy running the restaurant," I say, watching him and noticing the blush that spreads across his face.

"Um, can you give her my phone number? I would ask for hers, but in this day and age, you never know someone's intent, so it's better I just give her mine."

"How about you ask her yourself?" I say, coming up with an idea in the spur of the moment.

"How could I do that?"

"My family is having a retirement for my GrandPeter's wife and you can come as my guest. That will give you the ability to be around her and ask her for your number yourself."

"You'd do that?"

"Yeah, why not?" I ask, knowing he will be around all the Gideon men so Praise will be safe.

"Thank you, Skai, I'd love to,"

"Great," I say, and I give him the particulars and we agree to meet outside at a set time. With that done, he leaves the office and I go back to going over Cole's stats and planning my trip. They have a ferry that takes you to British Columbia Canada, and I book a ticket for that, too. I just need some time away and to stay too busy to think of him. I shut my computer and head home to pack.

JABARRI

I am irritated as hell. I miss the hell out of her but she is being unreasonable with this Natalie thing.

"Hey, Jabby, try this," Jaasiel says, walking into my office with a plate of something that smells amazing.

"I thought I asked you all to stop calling me that stupid-ass name," I snap.

"What the fuck did you do?" he asks me, making me even more irritated.

"Why does it automatically have to be something I did?" I retort and then catch what he says. "You knew?"

"Jabby," he calls me the nickname again, letting me know to pump my damn breaks. Jaasiel is the quietest one of us, but he might be the scariest and craziest. When he caught up to the man who abducted and tortured his wife, the hell Jaasiel unleashed had us all giving him the side eye. "The rest of our brothers may be too busy in their lives to notice the changes in you, but not me." Jaasiel and I have always been closer than the other brothers, so it doesn't surprise me that I am not hiding anything from him. So I give him the quick rundown without betraying Natalie's secret and how I feel Skai is being unreasonable.

"Hmm, so you're also basically having your cake and eating it too?"

"What? No? I told you Natalie and I are just friends,"

"Yeah, I heard you, but you are keeping your friendship with her not changing the dynamics of it and being with Skai without a real commitment, getting all the perks without making any sacrifices for it. And you really think that it's cool and that Skai would continue to accept that arrangement? You're not that stupid are you?"

"There's a lot you don't know, okay,"

"Man fuck outta here! Save that shit for someone else, you're fucking up. Who is more important, Jabarri, and don't say both because NO ONE should be on Skai's level in your life. Not a friend, not a sister, not even your mother. No one comes before Parker, period, and I would never let anyone think they are or could be. You have been pining away for Skai for years, and you are going to tell me you are willing to lose her to save a friendship? And newsflash, if Natalie was as good of a friend as you seem to think she is, she wouldn't put you in a position to lose Skai. Now try this," he says, shoving the spoon in my mouth. I chew the food, it's delicious but that is not surprising. "Amazing," I mumble out between chews.

"Yeah, I thought so, too," he says, turning on his heels and walking out, leaving his words ringing in my mind. I grab my keys to head out, I have to see her, but first, I check her location. She blocked her location from me, which may work with everyone else but not with me. I turn the location back on and notice she is in Seattle? Fuck. Well, I'll have to catch her at Lennox's party. I think about what Jaasiel says, and I know Skai and I need to talk. Hopefully, we can after the party. One thing he and I can agree on is that I waited too long to have her to fuck up and lose her.

Skai

Seattle was just what I needed, the atmosphere, the food, the people, it was wonderful, and I am not even going to talk about my trip to Victoria, British Columbia, stunning. I had an afternoon at a beautiful hotel, and struck up a conversation with a few other diners and ended up staying until it was time to board the ferry to go back to Seattle. And yes, Shepp was right. The hotel, gorgeous, but the amenities it offered made it easily one of the top three hotels I have ever been too. I was able to find a new dress for tonight's party and I can't wait to wear it, and I got Cole to come to the college this fall. Overall it was a successful trip, but even with all that Jabarri stayed on my mind the entire time.

I look at myself in the mirror, and like what I see, the dress fits better on me than it did when I tried it on in the store. I have my hair pulled up into my signature topknot bun, my make-up is full glam, and the heels have my short legs looking long, toned, and sexy. I hurry to grab my clutch and get out of the door so I can meet Elias on time. I had the Jeep washed and detailed while I was away, and she sparkled like a black diamond. I slide behind the steering wheel, press start, and listen to her roar to life. I hit my playlist and head towards the venue.

I spot Elias immediately. As soon as I come to a stop, the valet is at my door helping me out and handing me a ticket for my car.

"Coach, you look amazing," he says, taking me in from top to bottom, and I return the favor.

"As do you," I tell him, meaning it. "You clean up nice." And he does, his black floral textured jacket with the shawl-style lapel over the black slim-style pants are a perfect fit.

"I try," he says, the tips of his ears turning beet red. Looping my arm through the offered elbow, we make our way inside. "I came all this way and I don't know if I will have the courage to say anything to her." He is so cute and Praise couldn't find a better man.

"Praise is real cool and down to earth, but if you want a safe topic to broach her with, talk about cooking, and I promise she will open up and talk your ear off,"

"Thanks, Skai," he says my name, and it kinda takes me by surprise, there are times that the staff calls me coach so much that I wonder if they even remember my first name at all.

"No problem." We walk in the ballroom, and I direct Elias to the table with my mom and the rest of the ladies. Luckily for Elias, Saint begins talking to him, and he ends up hanging with them, and before long it's time for us to do our surprise performance. We have a ball, and Lennox is so entertained and happy all the hours rehearsing were worth it. And then, like the interlopers they are, the guys surprise us with performances of their own. And even though they are quite entertaining, there is one thing in here that has kept my attention all night, and that is Jabarri over there with Natalie. I want to make a scene, but I refuse to give him that much. I asked him not to bring her, and what did he do? He brings her. Deep down, I expected him to rectify the situation, and I guess he did, just not how I expected him to. I stand in the corner, going back and forth, watching what is going on in the ballroom and watching them. I crack a small smile when I see Elias and Praise sitting at a secluded table talking. *Well at least tonight worked out for one of us*, I think before my eyes swing back to him.

"What's wrong, little sis?" Brooklyn asks when she stands next to me.

"Nothing," I snap, but she follows my eyes to where I am looking, and end up looking at Jabarri and Natalie.

"You can't do that, Skai, He watched you be with someone for years. You can't get an attitude now that he is dating," she tells me.

"Hmp," I say, finally tearing my eyes off of Jabarri and Natalie.

"That is a completely different situation."

"How Skai? That man has had it bad for you for years, and you did not give him the time of day, so now that he has moved on and you're single, you still expect him to be there. That's not fair."

"You have it all figured out, huh?" I say, showing way more anger than I intend to.

"Skai," she tries.

"No, I was in a relationship, in what I thought was a happy relationship. I wasn't supposed to give him the time of day."

"Okay, and now?" she asks.

"Like I said, you have it all figured out, right? You have no idea what you are talking about, no idea at all. I have all the reasons to have a problem with what I am seeing over there."

"How Skai?"

"You know things aren't always what they seem. I would think someone like you would understand that because you and Aryan are damn sure more than just fucking friends," I tell her before walking away from her before I say even more than I intend to. I don't bother saying bye to Elias since he is knee-deep in a conversation with Praise, or anyone else. I head to the valet station, collect my car, and head home. I'm done with today.

Jabarri

I look around the ballroom and no longer see her, but I see the guy she came with sitting and talking to Praise. When she walked in here with him, I can't describe the anger and jealousy I felt. I noticed early on that her date had gone off with Praise, but that did not take away the jealousy I felt seeing her able to walk in here freely on the arm of another man. *Is that how she feels about me and Natalie?* I think. Was I really that clueless about how my friendship made her feel? I mean, no one but her knows it's just a friendship, and is Natalie taking advantage of our friendship? Shit, I have some things to think about. I want to go to her tonight. I have missed her so much, missed being in the house with her, sleeping in her bed, and her putting her cold-ass feet on me to warm them up. I just miss her. Natalie's voice finally breaks through my thoughts, and I realize she has been talking to me the entire time and I had completely blocked her out. And was her voice always this irritating? Yeah, I need to make some changes but I can't do it here at this party tonight. I focus back on Natalie and will the night to hurry and be over.

"Jabarri, you have been zoned out since Skai left,"

"Have I?"

"Yes, why don't you just go to her?"

"Because I can't go to her right now. There are a few things I need to do first," I tell her, not elaborating any further.

"Is there anything I can do to help?"

"Naw, not right now," I tell her. "Uh oh, it looks like they are about to turn this into a real party," I tell her as I watch the staff rearrange to tables so there is a large dance floor as the live band takes the stage. "You said you wanted to dance tonight," I remind her.

"I do. When you told me which band was going to be here, I knew I had to come. I love them. This is the perfect night. I am here with you and one of my favorite local bands. I can't think of anything better," she says as she pulls her phone out. The band begins to play as she taps the screen, her face immediately splitting into a smile. "Um, Jabarri, I gotta go,"

"Wait, what?" I ask in disbelief.

"Scottlyn sent a car for me, she wants me to come to her house right now. Sorry," she tells me as she kisses me on the cheek and practically runs out of the room so she can go see her girlfriend. I stand there dumbfounded, she really just ditched me.

"And that's what you are sacrificing Skai for? She just abandoned you? At your family's event? Yeah, I can see why you'd be more loyal to her," Jaasiel says, walking away, his words making me grind my teeth together. Tomorrow I will talk to Natalie and then I am going to go after Skai, again.

The party was great. I stayed and partied with my family until we finally called it a night. This morning, I woke up with a plan to go see Natalie and talk to her about how things need to change, but instead, I get a text from her telling me to stay away from her house because she's told her parents that I have taken her away on an impromptu trip. In reality, she is on an impromptu trip with Scottlyn for the week. Well, ain't that a bitch. I wouldn't dare go to Skai half-assed so I guess I have to wait a week.

Skai

It has been a little more than a week since the party, and no Jabarri. I thought I was hurt by Alayna but his indifference is killing me. I have had to stop myself from going to the compound and confronting him, but I refuse to do it. I grab my notebook and prepare to get some work done tonight so I can have a jump on work tomorrow, when the doorbell rings. I hate my stupid ass heart. It immediately jumps, hoping it's Jabarri. I hurry to the door and practically skid to a stop when I see not Jabarri on my doorstep but Brooklyn.

"Brooklyn?"

"Skai," she says, her voice breaking right before tears begin to flow down her face. I reach for her, and she breaks down even more. She finally gets herself together, and we make it in the door to the living room.

"What happened?" I ask, and when she tells me what happened, I am pissed.

"Uncle Aryan is going to make me beat his ass! You can stay here for as long as you need. Do you want the upstairs or downstairs guest room?"

"I'll take the upstairs room," she says.

I lead her upstairs to the room and leave her to get settled. "If you want to talk more or just want to sit without talking, I'll be in my room. Come on down," I tell her before walking out. Almost an hour later, there is a knock on my door,

"Come in," I yell through the door. She walks in as I am cleaning up and hanging my clothes in the closet. She climbs up in my bed, grabs a pillow, and hugs it as she watches me move about the room.

"I am sorry, Skai, for assuming the night of the retirement party."

"I understand, let's just let it go," I say quickly, grabbing the remote and turning on the TV to some true crime drama as I crawl into the bed and start working on my paperwork until we both fall asleep listening to why the woman on the screen killed her husband.

CHAPTER 9

*J*abarri

You have got to be kidding me! I think when I hear Aryan complaining about Brooklyn actually leaving him…finally. I am happy she finally put her foot down, but why the hell did she have to find refuge with Skai at Skai's house? It's been a couple of weeks, and nothing has changed, but today, we are helping Brooklyn pack her stuff up and moving her out of Aryan's suites. That means she is finally alone and Natalie has been avoiding me but that shit stops today! It's quick work to get Brooklyn all set up in her new house, and I am heading straight to talk to Natalie. I didn't bother calling first and giving her the chance to avoid me and I pull into her driveway, get out the car and walk in the house without bothering to knock. I catch her and Scottlyn kissing on the sofa, jumping apart guiltily.

"You're in here doing that and left the front door open? I could have very easily been your parents walking in here,"

"Jabarri, what's wrong?" she asks, jumping up from the sofa.

"We need to talk."

"Can't it wait?"

"No, we need to talk. Now." I tell her.

"I'm going to go so y'all can talk. I'll call you later," Scottlyn says, grabbing her keys and leaving.

"It's time, Natalie. You were supposed to tell your parents weeks ago, but you haven't."

"You know why, Jabarri. I thought you'd understand you haven't told your family about Skai either. What's the difference?"

"The difference is you haven't had to choose between me or Scottlyn. The difference is I never put you in a position where you could lose what you have with her, but you have constantly done that for me. It's ninety percent my fault because I let you, but you were okay with my losing Skai as long as you got to be with Scottlyn and not upset your family,"

"I'll lose everything," she whispers as the first tear falls.

"You won't lose me, Nat. But I can't keep being this person for you. I want my happily ever after, too. Things between us have to change,"

"I know, and I am sorry. As much as my family drives me to drink, I can't imagine losing them. They are all I have,"

"You won't lose me, sis," Camryn says from the doorway.

"You heard?" she says to her brother on the verge of freaking out.

"Yeah, I heard, but honestly, I knew you liked girls,"

"What! How?"

"It wasn't that hard to spot, and if Mom and Dad stopped riding in the boat on the river of denial, they'd be able to admit they knew, too. Listen, we can't keep living our lives to please Mom and Dad. Someone has to break this controlling cycle we've been living in, and why not us? I am leaving, I have my own dreams and desires, and I am going to live my life. I have been saving for years, and I have enough saved to go live in Europe for several years." He reaches into the bag he was holding and pulls out a phone box. "Here's a phone for you. I paid it for the year, which should give you enough time to find a job and be able to pay for it on your own. Get some independence, Nat. Depending and relying on Mom and Dad is what got us into this mess, and I am over it. I love you, sis," he tells her, pulling her into a tight hug.

"You're leaving me?"

"Come with me,"

"I can't, Scottlyn is here. I love her,"

"Well, you two can come visit me,"

"Yes, we can. When do you leave?"

"As soon as my passport gets here," he says, and her eyes widen with the news.

"You got a passport? How did you do that without Mom and Dad knowing?"

"Like I said, I saved my money, I got a PO Box, and a separate phone, and one day when they were away, I had my own internet ran so they couldn't monitor what I was researching. This shit isn't normal, Nat, none of this is. We're both adults, but they treat us worse than toddlers.

My passport will come to the PO Box, and I will buy my airline ticket and leave. Hell, I keep a go bag in my trunk."

"Will you at least let me see you before you just leave?"

"Of course, that is why I got you your own phone. But Jabarri is right. It's time to stop living in fear, and it's not right to keep him from having the life he's been waiting for, just like it's not right for you to not be able to live your life." he hugs her again before kissing her forehead. "Can you keep an eye out for her?"

"Certainly. I wish you the best," I tell him, shaking his hand before he walks out.

"You know you don't have to tell them shit, just move out. I have a couple of houses that are available. We can go tomorrow and take a look at them," I offer her.

"Okay," she says, and I take a deep breath. It feels like I am finally able to breathe. *Hold on, Skai, I'm coming! And this time, I am not leaving,*

SKAI

"Oh, uh, no thanks. I'm married," I tell the guy who is trying to ask me out on a date. All I wanted was a frappucino and I am being hounded. Ugh, I hate it here. I kinda wondered if I liked all men, but nope, just one in particular. Men still give me the ick.

"Where's your ring then?"

"Being cleaned," I respond without thinking as I pick up my speed to get away from him because the next stop is shooting his ass, and admittingly he is a nice-looking man, he's just not my man.

"Whatever," he says, finally turning and walking away. Thank God. I get in my car and take off before he changes his mind. Brooklyn is all set up in her house, and once again, I am alone. What's crazy is I have always enjoyed being alone, actually preferred it, but since Jabarri and Brooklyn left, the house just feels extra lonely now. I don't bother pulling into the garage when I get home and come to find out that was a mistake. I feel him as soon as I cross the threshold, I can sense him, can smell him. I round the corner, and there he is, sprawled out on my sofa.

"Get out," I tell him without preamble, heading to my bedroom. *Please leave, please leave, please leave.* I chant in my head because he picked the day where I am feeling the most fragile. If he touches me, I am going to fold like a lawn chair.

"Skai, I just want to talk, please," he says as he reaches for me, and I almost roll my ankle avoiding contact.

"I can't touch you or talk to you now,"

"Jabarri, just say what you want to say and get out,"

"Damn. Well, okay, I know I made a mess of this trying to be a friend for Natalie and be there for you, but I realize now that there was no way I could do both and I am sorry that you took the most loss in the situation. I talked to Natalie. I won't lose you, Skai, not when I just got you,"

"Who says I am still available or want to be with you anymore? It felt kinda nice going to the party with Elias,"

"Don't play with me, Skai! You almost got Elias archived," he says, and I am forced to hold in the laugh even though I know he is serious.

"You're being a bit dramatic, aren't you? I was doing him a favor. There is nothing there but friendship, but I still enjoyed being on a man's arm."

"Let me explain something to you," he starts.

"No, there is nothing to explain, Jabarri. You made a choice and whatever happens as a result of that choice, is of your own making. You are not about to stand here and act like a neanderthal from the thought of me being with someone else. If you wanted me and didn't want anyone else to be with me then you should have acted like it. Now if that is all you have to say we're done here and I am sure you can find your way out," I turn on my heels to put as much space between us as possible.

"You know, Skai," he says moving slowly toward me like I am a skittish horse. "You have been going out of your way to avoid me touching you." He continues advancing on me until his front is pressed against my front. Even though I did not want him touching me, I am no punk or coward. There is no way I was going to run from him.

"You're touching me now, Ja bar ri," I say, purposely emphasizing the syllables in his name. "I'm not running," I tell him, craning my neck to look up at him. In all the time we were together, we have kept everything pretty PG, simply due to my hang-ups, but I got a feeling tonight is going to change that. Am I nervous? Yes. Am I comfortable with men? No, not sexually. If he touches me, will I stop him? No. Out of all the men on this planet, I crave him, I want to feel him feel me, every part of me.

But I am supposed to stand firm for all the bull shit he put me through with his stupidity, right? *Yes, damn it, Skai, the answer is yes, but... shit, fuck it.* And that is the last coherent thought I had before I feel his hand on my face seconds before his lips touch mine lightly, exploring, asking permission, and just like I thought, my willpower exits stage left. My hands burrow in his hair, as I open my mouth to his gentle assault, that turns almost frantic. We groan at the same time, the kiss becomes more intense. I grab handfuls of his hair pulling and he returns the favor by grabbing a handful of my ass and squeezing. The next thing I know I am in the air, my legs wrapped around his waist and the wall at my back. Somewhere in the background I wait for the panic to set in, but all I feel is him. I undulate my hips rubbing my legging covered pussy against the bulge in his pants chasing the orgasm that is barreling down on me. In my relationship with Alayna, I was the aggressive one, the one who controlled what happened in the bedroom, and Jabarri is going to have to accept that he can't control me in or out of the bedroom.

"That's cute, Skai," he tells me once he releases my mouth.

"Hush, you're breaking my concentration," I tell him, doubling my effort to cum. "What wait! No! Jabarri, why would you do that!" I am practically screaming from the loss of him and the orgasm that I was seconds away from.

"You need to learn something, Skai,"

"Now? I need to learn it right now? Are you crazy? Save this shit for later, preferably after I cum. Do you know how long it's been?"

"Yeah, since you were born, because regardless of what you thought of sex before me, trust me I am going to redefine it for you. And you're not about to use me like a human vibrator to get off on, I control what happens in the bedroom, Skai, not you."

"Pfft," I reply.

"Challenge accepted."

"What?" I ask, and he is setting me on my feet. As soon as my feet touch the floor, he moves back just enough to spin me to face the wall, his chest pressing against my back, and pressing me against the wall.

"Who are you with, Skai?"

"You."

"What's. My. Name?"

My God, was being with an aggressively dominating man on my bingo card this year? No, it was not, but, damn, I'm glad it is now.

"Jabarri,"

"Damn right! You remember that. Remember that I will always protect you and I will never hurt you. You. Are. Mine! And I will kill anyone and anything that threatens that or you, I will. Do you trust me?"

"Yes," comes out on a choked breath when I feel his hand push past the band of my leggings and touch my soaked lips.

"Fuck you are wet, baby. Is this all for me?" he asks, and I can't put two words together to come up with any kind of response, so I simply answer with a shake of my head. "Use your words, Nöku Ahi."

"Your fire? Yes, it's all for you, Taku Rangimārie," his finger separates my lips to find and rub my clit. Immediately, my legs give out, his other arm bands around me to hold me in place as he continues to manipulate my body and give me the pleasure I need. "Hands on the wall," he growls in my ear. I want to hear you enjoy this, Skai. I want your cries to fill my ears as my fingers fill your tight channel. Can you do that for me, baby? I like words of affirmation so I know I am doing a good job. *Harder, Jabarri. More, Jabarri. Yes, Jabarri. I'm cumming, Jabarri,* and my personal favorite, *I love you, Jabarri.*"

Damn, the man is killing me. I am hanging on by a thread. I am literally fighting back from cumming just out of spite. I am such a fucking brat.

"Oh, you're fighting it," he says, biting my collarbone before I feel his finger slide inside me with precision and my muscles clamp down immediately on the digit. The heel of his hand is pressed against my nubbin as he begins pumping his finger in and out of me. He pulls the finger out and replaces it with two, then three, while consistently manipulating my clit. When I cum, I am going to black out.

"Give it to me, Skai. Let your body go. I got you. Let me hear the pleasure I'm giving you. I love the feel of you, inside and out, just for me. Only for me. I can't wait to fuck you properly, to push inside of you, and feel your heat wrapped around my dick. I waited so many years for you, and the first time I fuck you is going to feel like perfection. Damn, I've missed you. I love you so fucking much, now stop being stubborn and cum."

I turn my face to rest my cheek on the wall to try to get a look at him and let go of the tight hold I had on my body. "Aaahhhhh!" I scream as I orgasm, making my mind shut down. I turn my face to see him, and all I see is white light and hear roaring in my ears. After a long few seconds, I hear his voice filter through the noise. "I got you, baby. I love you. Fuck, you're beautiful," and then nothing.

CHAPTER 10

*J*abarri

My arm is stiff as hell from holding it in the same position, but it's a small price to pay to hold a naked Skai in my arms all night. After the hallway incident, I carried her to her bedroom and laid her on her bed before going to the bathroom to wet a washcloth to clean her up. She ruined her leggings and panties when she squirted. I peeled the wet clothing from her body, threw them in the wash, cleaned her up, stripped, and joined her in bed. Even in her sleep, she got as close to me as humanly possible, and I was more than happy to hold her close to me as we both fell asleep. I really wasn't expecting what happened. I really came to just talk, but when I saw how much she was avoiding me touching her, I knew I had to do just that. And I don't regret it for a single millisecond. I feel the change as soon as it happens. "Good morning," I say, kissing her forehead.

"How did you know I was awake?" she asks into my side, her eyes still closed.

"Your breathing changed," I answer honestly. "Are you ready to talk this morning?"

"I guess," she says, and I can feel her body stiffen.

"Relax, Skai, it's just me and you here. Let's talk this out, okay?"

"Okay," she says, and I feel her relax a fraction.

"I talked to Natalie and explained to her that I can no longer do things the way we were doing them. That you are my priority, and I would still be there for her but not at the expense of you. She is planning on telling her parents and we've already picked out a house for her to move to. I need you to be okay with things, Skai. I won't be away from you again."

"I never wanted or expected you to not be her friend or help her, Barbie. I had a problem with her calling on you all hours of the night, and you would get up out of my bed and go running. It was other things, too, but the fact that you consistently put her first was a problem for me. I didn't feel it was fair because it was never the other way; you never put me before her. Hell, I would've felt better if we were at least equal, but I didn't even feel that," she says, and I feel ashamed because as much as I didn't want to admit it before, she was right.

"I am sorry, Skai, I won't ever do that again if you plan on keeping me in your life,"

"Um, didn't you say last night that I was yours?"

"I did,"

"Well, okay then,"

"Then let's go talk to your mom and my brother,"

"Uh, pump your breaks on that one. First, we have to get Natalie settled, and we have to find our footing again before dealing with the fall out of my mom and your brother. DJ ain't wrapped all that tight," she says, and she has all valid points.

"Well, let me tell her to get a damn move on so we can just focus on us,"

"This is going to change everything for her. How does she think her brother is going to take it?" she asks, and I tell her everything that happened between Natalie and her brother.

"Well damn, he's been planning his exit plan all this time,"

"He has, and as soon as his passport comes, he is out of here," I tell her when my phone chirps. I manage to reach my phone without having to move away from Skai.

"Is that her?"

"Yeah, she basically telling me she is telling her parents tonight at dinner,"

"Oh damn, does she want you there,"

"No, she said this is something she needs to handle on her own,"

"Wow. I still feel like you shouldn't make any plans so you can be ready to go help her if she needs you," she says, and I realize even more that she didn't have a problem with my relationship with Natalie. She had a problem with what that friendship was causing problems with us. "Maybe I will. Now, enough about Natalie, what do you want to do today?"

"Can we just stay in bed all day?"

"Oh, for sure," I tell her because I can't think of many better ways to spend the day. We ordered in food, barely got out of the bed, watched TV and talked the entire day away. The sun began to set, and as soon as the sun set, his phone began blowing up with notification chirps.

"Shit, she told them," I say, relaying to Skai what is going on in my messages.

"Damn, her father damn near choked on his steak,"

"Her mother broke out in hysterical crying." I am reading the messages as fast I can, but the amount coming in has me behind.

"Wow, her mother asked her to simply stop being attracted to women."

"Her father said she was going to hell,"

"Her mother said that her mother's neighbor's granddaughter had the lesbian, and she just stopped being that way one day,"

"I'm sorry, what?"

"Oh, here we go. She told her parents there is no changing who she is and that Scottlyn is her romantic partner for platonic friend, and her father said she is dead to him,"

"Uh oh she sent a voice note this time," I tell her, put the phone on speaker and press play.

"When I told them the truth and refused to give in to their demands, they basically told me to get out of their house and that I was cut off. So I told

them fuck you, and I've already moved out. I also told them that I'm glad that you have each other since you won't have any of your children or grandchildren. And I told them that I hope they die together because neither Camryn nor I will be around to take care of their old asses. Then I got up and left. Oh, by the way, Camryn is gone and I moved in with Scottlyn. So thanks for the house but we won't be needing it. Tell Skai sorry and thanks, and if you two are up for it, let's do a double date. Oh, and Scottlyn thinks since I came out to my family, it's time you two come out to yours! Love y'all, bye!"

"Wow," we both say.

"So what do you think? Time to talk to our family?" I ask her.

"Uh, no. Let's not get carried away," she says immediately, which makes me laugh.

"What would you do if our family doesn't want us together?"

"Just ask what you're really asking, Jabarri. What if my mom and your brother don't want us together?"

"Yeah, what then?"

"Honestly, I have no idea. My mother has never denied me anything, ever, so I would be in uncharted territory. Truthfully, if I am happy, my mother would be okay with almost anything, but you are a Gideon, Jabarri. There aren't really much better than y'all. I'm just not sure I am ready to let our family into what we have especially since we are just getting back on track. Let's get our footing first and then talk about this," she says, and she has a lot of valid points. Her whole argument is logical, so I simply say.

"Okay. I have a question,"

"What is it?"

"Can you get a few days off work?"

"Probably not, but if you are trying to take me out of town, I can make it a work trip there are a couple of recruits I could go talk to,"

"Where?"

"Um, it depends. Do we want to stay close or go far?"

"Far,"

"There's a recruit in California,"

"How long would you need to do your thing?"

"A day, maybe two, and if I want to stay longer, I can,"

"How long?"

"A couple of days,"

"Yeah that'll work. Let's plan it," We spend the rest of the day planning the trip.

SKAI

Jabarri shakes me awake when the town car pulls up to the hotel. After his idea to go away for a couple of days, everything went pretty fast. I texted Saint and let him know my plans so he could call the family and set up the meeting with the Coopers. Another text to Shepp had the hotel secured, and Jabarri had us booked on an early morning flight. I don't have to meet with the Coopers until tomorrow, so I plan on getting to this room and getting straight in bed. On top of being up at the crack of dawn the time change has me on the verge of collapse. I check-in, and they offer to take our bags up, but Jabarri declines, opting to carry them instead. As soon as the door is open, I walk in, stripping as I go until I reach the bedroom. Pulling back the covers, I literally fall into the bed and am asleep before my head actually touches the pillow. In my sleep-addled mind I think about how far I have come stripping in front of Jabarri with comfort and ease. I faintly registered him joining me in bed and pulling me into his arms before I got carried back off to sleep.

I woke up late and ravenous. I slept the entire day away yesterday, and when my eyes finally opened, I was running late for my meet, and my stomach was gnawing away at my backbone for nourishment. I hustle getting dressed, and rush out of the room, but not before Jabarri pushes a breakfast sandwich and a bottle of orange juice in my hand as I pass through the door. I make it just in time to not be late for the meeting and realize this was a waste as soon as I talk to the family. Although the kid has talent, his attitude is terrible and entitled as are his parents. Since Saint took over the football program at Hillwood University, aka the southern HU, he has won every College Football National Championship by stacking his team with talent but also using and instilling young men with an amazing work ethic, drive, and sense of teamwork.

All this kid and his family are thinking about is money, sponsorships, and how much he touches the ball. They actually had the nerve to say he has to be in possession of the ball at least twelve of the fifteen minutes of each quarter of the game. Like damn, when does anyone else get a chance to play? I wrapped the meeting up and left. I feel sorry for any team that gets this Prima Donna for their team, but he won't be a Titan any time soon.

To my surprise, instead of the car taking me back to the hotel, it is en route to the airport. I texted Jabarri in the middle of the meeting that I was going to be wrapping up soon, so I guess he figured we could start our trip a little earlier than planned. He is waiting for me when the car pulls up to the curb and helps me out of the car as soon as it comes to a stop. He has already checked in and checked the bags, but I need to check in, and that is when I find out we are heading to Molokai. Lord, the time change from Mississippi almost took me out, but now we're going to Hawaii? My body is never going to recover. Hawaii is five hours earlier than the time in Mississippi. I'm going to sleep on the plane. Jabarri carries me into the hotel this time because I refuse to move, and back in the bed I go. It was a five-hour flight back in time. When we left California, it was four post-meridiem, which is six in Mississippi, and now here in Hawaii, it's freaking one post meridiem. My body doesn't know what to do.

SKAI

"Wake up, baby," I hear.

"Leave me alone,"

"You gotta eat, or you are going to get a migraine. Then you can go back to sleep because I have a lot planned for us tomorrow,"

"Fine," I grumble waking up long enough to eat and go right back to sleep. By the time morning rolls around I am well rested and ready to go. I leave Jabarri in bed, as I head to the bathroom to get ready for the day. I throw on a crop top tee shirt and some leggings with my sandals. I pull my braids up in high bun and through on some light makeup and lip gloss and I am ready for whatever Jabarri has planned.

I hear a deep breath behind me, making me turn to see Jabarri standing there looking good as hell and irritated. "What's wrong?"

"You just want me to catch a charge. Why are you naked,"

"I have on clothes, Jabarri,"

"Is that what you call it? I can see your belly button piercing, and since you have on no bra, I can clearly see your dagger nipple rings. And as soon as someone looks too long or makes a comment, I'm going to have to fuck someone up,"

"Possessive much?"

"I'm a Gideon," he says like that explains it all, and honestly, it does.

"I can change," I offer.

"Nope, I want you to wear what you want. I'll try to control myself," He says, walking past me. "In more ways than one."

An hour later, and we are in a jeep going up a mountain to God knows where. We go zip lining, whale watching, then take ATV's up the volcano.

"Are you enjoying yourself?"

"Today was amazing!" I tell him as the sun moves across the sky in preparation for setting.

"The day isn't over, come on," he takes my hand as we walk towards a building that I didn't realize is a spa. We are shown to our room and given the chance to undress for our massage. We get undressed and lay on the table, waiting for our massage therapists to come in. I am not at all surprised when a man and woman walk in. The man works on him, and the woman on me. After all of the activities that we did today, this massage is a godsend, and he and I are both a boneless mass of flesh when they are done. They leave us in the room when they are done to give us time to get dressed.

"This is the best day that I have had in a long time, Skai,"

"Mmm, me, too. Thank you for suggesting a trip and bringing me here,"

"Well, it's not like we can hang out at home unless we want our families to know,"

"True, but you didn't have to bring me to Hawaii to take me out though,"

"True. Come on, the day isn't over. And if I know you, I know your bottomless pit is hungry,"

"Kiss my ass," I tell him as I scoot off the bed. "Aahhhh!" I scream when his arms reach out and circle my waist before pulling me back to him, still lying on the table. He pulls my blanket away, pulls my panties down, and kisses my ass before giving it a lite bite. Then he pulls my panties back up, slaps my ass and pushes me towards my clothes.

"Don't threaten me with a good time, Skai," he says, sitting up and swinging his legs off of the side of the table. I am back in his arms as soon as he is close to me. He simply holds me, but then his mouth is on mine.

"Come on before I say fuck it and have my way with you on one of these tables,"

"I mean," I start because even though I wasn't before, I am ready now. Ready to be his completely.

"Come on, you cheap floozy, let's get out here before you defile me and take advantage of my virtue," he says, pulling his shirt collar together in mock horror and I burst out laughing.

"Virtue, my ass," I tell him. "But I am hungry, so I'll let it go for now," I tell him as I push my feet in my shoes, and he gets dressed. We head back to the hotel, shower, and get dressed for dinner. I can remember listening to my mom talk about the dates that DJ took her on, how different and special they were but never in a million years did I think I would be experiencing it for myself. We are having dinner behind a waterfall. There is a table, flowers, candles, and a chef. The air is scented with Plumeria since they are littered every-where, providing the perfect backdrop. He pulls out a chair for me before taking his own seat. "Jabarri, this is crazy," I say, looking over the rail. It's the only thing keeping us from falling at least forty feet into the water. The sun is going down and the reds and gold reflect off of the clear blue water.

"Are you happy?"

"Yes," I say, looking at him as he takes my hand across the table. The chef serves us dinner, and Jabarri feeds me never breaking eye contact. It is one of the most intimate, intense things I have ever experienced. "Open," he would say, and I would have to remember he was talking about my mouth and not my legs, and that would lead me to wonder why he wasn't talking about my legs, too. Soon dinner is over and the servers clear all the food and plates away, leaving just him and I and out of nowhere music begins playing low. I don't want to move or talk or break this spell that he has weaved for us tonight.

JABARRI

"You're stunning, even more now than when I first met you. There were so many moments that I thought I would never get the chance to be with you. So many days, I would long to be the one who shared your life and love, who cared for you and made you happy. I had given up on us altogether, and I started dating, and then I met Natalie," I tell her, rubbing her face as I go back over our history. "The night you came to the house crying because you caught Alayna with another woman in your house, in your bed, made me want to go on a killing spree. But deep down I was happy, not happy that you were hurt, but for the first time, I had a chance for us to be together. However, now I was the one with the hold-up, Natalie. And I wanted to give you a chance to heal, and even after all of that I still almost fucked this up. I promised myself that if we got past that, I wouldn't take you or us for granted. I love you so much and for so long, Skai. I can't live without you anymore, and I am not perfect and I might mess up but I promise to always listen to you and always try to do better, to be better for you, for my wife," I tell her and opened the box she didn't even notice that I pulled out. She slaps both hands over her mouth as a tear races down her face.

"Jabarri," she whispers.

"Talk to me, Nöku Ahi. Is that a yes?"

"Our family?"

"What about them? This is about me and you, Skai. Tell me, baby, will you be my wife?"

"Yes," she says so softly I almost don't hear it over the roar of the waterfall. I slip the three-row round diamond eternity wedding band on her finger.

"I got a flat ring because I didn't want the ring to get in the way of your job while you are out on the football field with your brother. But if you would prefer a more traditional style ring I'll get you a second ring to wear.

"This is perfect," she whispers and jumps up, coming over to me to hug me. She takes my face in both of her hands and kisses me. Things turn fast as I stand with her in my arms, setting her on the table. I stand in between her legs, kissing her, and she has my shirt in a death grip as I explore every inch of her mouth. I grip her thigh, sliding my hand up her silken thigh until I reach her panties.

"Please," she begs, ripping her mouth from mine. I pull down the top of her dress and capture her nipple in my mouth. I use my teeth to pull the nipple rings, wrenching out a moan from her. She cups the back of my head, holding my head to her nipple as if I planned on going anywhere. I switch breasts as I pull and manipulate the nipple ring of the other nipple. "Jabarri," she whines.

"Are you ready for me? I wanted to give you time, if you need more time, I am okay with that. We have the rest of our lives,"

"I need you, I want you."

"Hold on to me," she wraps her legs around my waist as I stand to my full height and walk towards the falls. I walk us through the blanket of water to the hidden alcove behind the water. A local told me about it earlier. It is completely hidden from view from the other side. I set her on a stone ledge, immediately dropping to my knees, flipping her dress up, and snatching her ass to the edge of the ledge. I push her panties to the side, and I dive in head first. My first taste of her has my head spinning; sweet nectar, like the rarest ambrosia, erupts across my taste buds. I grab her ass in both hands, lift her to my mouth, and devour her pussy like I am on death row and she is my last meal. All I hear on repeat in my head is Skai, Skai, Skai, my mind unable to comprehend the fact that I am here doing this with Skai. She has snatched my hair tie out of my head as she uses my hair like reins, directing where she wants me, and I am okay letting her be the navigator this time. Her shoes clank to the floor seconds before her feet are on my shoulders, opening her to me even more. I slip two fingers inside, stretching her getting her ready to accept my dick inside of her as I take her swollen nub back in my mouth, holding it between my teeth as my tongue flicks across it, bringing her to an explosive orgasm.

"Fuck, Jabarri," she moans, and I and already addicted to hearing her pleasure. "This is," she stops to catch her breath. "I, I don't know if I can do this. If I can take this," she pants out, and I remember that this will be her first real-time with a man, that alone forces me to slow down. I am so hard it hurts. I think I would cum just by her touching my dick. Standing to my full height, I unbuckle my pants, letting them fall and push down my boxer briefs, my heavy dick hanging ready, seeking her out.

"I got you, Skai. Do you trust me?" I ask, already knowing the answer. I wouldn't have gotten this close if she didn't trust me.

"You know I do,"

"We are here together, baby. We are enjoying together. Do you want this?" I ask, pulling back so I can look into her eyes.

"Yes," she answers, her eyes dropping to the ground.

"Look at me, Skai" I command, slowly her eyes find mine.

"I won't rush this. I won't push you. You don't have to say yes, baby. You are not obligated to do this. I will be fine with what we've already done,"

"Jabarri, you are obviously turned on," she says, her eyes dropping to my obvious erection.

"I am a grown man, baby. I won't die. But I don't want you doing shit you don't want to do out of obligation or fear. I want you to want to feel yourself stretched around my dick. I want you to crave cumming on my dick. I want you to brag about the way your cum is dripping off my balls. The same way I crave to be with you in any way. If you aren't ready, we will go back to our hotel and enjoy the rest of our mini vacation. So tell me, Skai, what do you want?" I ask, my dick still hard. I wait, barely breathing, waiting for her to let me know how this night is going to end. But she never answers me verbally. Instead, she grasps my dick with her slender fingers, and I almost buckle from the contact.

"Let's do this together," I tell her as she explores my dick with her hand, slowly stroking and caressing me in her soft palm. I grit my teeth against the urge to thrust and cum. I am so close to being on the edge. "You like him? He's yours, Nöku Ahi, anytime you want him. Can you feel how hard he is, how turned on you make me? Tell me, Skai, did you use a strap-on with her,"

"Yes,"

"Did it make you moan? Did you cum on it?"

"Jabarri," she moans, not answering the question. I pull the top of her dress down to expose her tight nipples to the cool, wet air right as I suck one in my mouth, pulling on her nipple ring. She almost drops my dick from the sensations I am causing her body to feel. I pull on her nipple, flicking it with my tongue before releasing it with a loud pop.

"That's not an answer, Skai,"

"Got damn, Jabarri, yes!"

"Hmm, that's cute, baby, if you could moan and cum from a fake dick, I am going to have you screaming, crying, and begging as your pussy grips and sucks on this one hundred percent real dick. I am going to show you why authentic beats imitation every single time. I am going to slut you out over this dick, baby, like I am already slutted out for that pussy, now put me where I need to be," I kiss her before she can respond, but I let her guide me to her. The first touch, and I am fighting not to push inside of her, letting her set the pace.

"Help me," she begs, but honestly, I don't think she needs any help as she rubs my dick up and down her wet pussy, using the head like a vibrator on her clit.

"Are you masturbating on my dick, baby?"

"Yes," she says, completely letting the feelings eliminate any embarrassment.

"Well then, get that shit, use my dick to get off on. Let me watch you cum from the pleasure I provide," I command. She doubles her effort. I pull my shirt off as I watch her, watching the pleasure reflect on her face until she throws her head back, screaming her climax. She slaps my chest before she grabs my neck, squeezing it as she rides the waves of her pleasure. "Ataahua, beautiful. Are you ready?"

"Yes," she pants out. I place the head at her opening with one hand and grab her jaw with the other, forcing her to look at me as I begin to push my way inside of her. *Shit!* I think. She is tight. I play with her clit to get her to relax and loosen up on me. Rocking my hips as I play with her clit, I go deeper with each thrust, taking my time and opening her up. I lean down to suck her bottom lip in my mouth. "Loosen up, love, let me inside. Come on, Skai, let's fuck each other. I want you to fuck yourself on my dick, baby."

"Stop talking, Jabarri,"

"No, talk back to me. Say what you want to say. I'm yours, Skai, and you're mine," I tell her as I fully seat myself inside of her. "That's what I'm talking about. I can feel you griping me. I dreamed about this with you for over eight years, and here we are. Fuck, I love you," I tell her as I pull almost out before sliding back in. I put her legs over my arms as I hold her ass in my hands, lifting her off the rock to hold her just how I want her as I begin fucking her hard.

"Together," I remind her. "Look at me," I demand. Pulling back to the tip before slamming back in.

"Don't leave me, stay with me,"

"I'm here," she says, taking her leg from the crook of my arm and putting it over my shoulder. She has finally loosened up. She locks her eyes on mine, and I know I am not going to last long. My thumb makes its way to her nub and circles. "Cum with me, Skai," I tell her as the telltale tinges at the base of my spine begin. I waited so long for this I can't hold back.

"I'm so close," she says between moans, and I readjust her in my arms, bending my knees, I thrust up, and she cums so fast and so hard the scream is ripped from her throat.

"Fuck yes, baby, cum all on me,"

"Cum in me, Jabarri," and I realize a couple of things at once. I am indeed going to cum inside of her, and we did not use any type of birth control, and I don't care. Skai is my wife, whether we've made it legal or not. "Cum for me, Jabarri. Show me how much you like being inside of me,"

"There she is! There's my naughty girl. I've been waiting to meet you," I push up again as she clamps down, and the cum shoots out of me so fast and unexpectedly that my legs almost give out on me, and I have to use the wall behind her to steady myself.

"Mmmm, looks like I am not the only one affected, after all, you did say we would do this together." Her and that smart-ass mouth, I think as I rest my forehead against hers as we both struggle to catch our breath. *I just fucked Skai!* I think, amazed by the fact that after all these years I got what I have desired most in my life.

CHAPTER 11

*S*kai

I can not believe what just happened! Not only did I sleep with a man, I slept with Jabarri! What the hell! After making love under the waterfall we got dressed and headed back to the hotel. If I thought Jabarri was tactile before it has multiplied exponentially now. He has to have some part of his body touching mine. If I wasn't sure if I was in love with him before I know I am now. Most men creep me out immediately, but with him, I want to be with him. I want him touching me, I feel safe with him, not just physically safe, but I can trust him with my heart and my trust, and I know he won't hurt or disappoint me. His hand is on my thigh as we ride back to the hotel. I lay my head back and fall right on to sleep. I didn't have to keep my eyes open, or be on the lookout, or navigate. Nope all I had to do was ride and be with him, and that is a new and frankly intoxicating feeling. I used to make fun of my mother for being like that with DJ, but I get it now. I am in my soft girl era, and I have no intention of ever going back to anything else.

When we reach the hotel, I sit there like I don't even know how to operate a door. I don't move until he comes around and opens the door to help me out of the car.

"If I had known all I needed to do was fuck you proper to get this side of you, I would have fucked you a lot sooner," he says in my ear as we walk in the hotel, and I blush like a high school girl with a crush.

"Shut up, Barbie, I still have my gun on me," I tell him.

"Yes, ma'am," he says.

"We have to tell your mom and my brother,"

"Do we have to?"

"Skai, baby, you know we do,"

"I have enjoyed keeping this between us, especially now. How is the family going to take this?"

"I know. Me too, but with our family, it is unrealistic to think we can keep this a secret. And even though my other brothers have made fun of me over the years and even offered advice, will they actually feel that way when we confirm we are together? I mean, I am your uncle, by the way,"

"Get the fuck out of here! You were never my uncle. I never felt that with you. If I am being honest, I never once felt uncle niece relationship with you. Besides, I was a grown adult when my mom married your brother. So that shit doesn't count," I tell him, but deep down, I know some people will feel like this relationship is inappropriate. I just dare one of them to say it to my face. Although if we get married my uncles will also be my brother-in-laws and my mom will be my mom and sister-in-law! Yeah, that's weird as hell.

Our trip is over faster than I would have liked, and we are on our way back home and back to reality. I look at the ring that he proposed to me with, and I still can't wrap my head around the fact that I am engaged to Jabarri Manaia Gideon.

"Do you like your ring? You keep looking at it,"

"I love it."

"When do you want to tell our family?"

"Umm…" I hedge.

"Mrs. Gideon, I am sure they will be fine with it and happy for us."

"Really? So you're ready to talk to my mom and DJ? How do you think that conversation will go?"

"I am a Gideon, baby, you can't get better than us for a husband."

"Wow," I say, not at all impressed.

"Seriously, for as long as I have desired you, I am sure they'll be fine. It might be an adjustment period, but things will be fine,"

"Ok, but can we enjoy this just between us for a little while longer?"

"Of course, Nōku Ahi. But I just want to warn you Jaasiel knows," he says as they place our bags in the trunk and we slide in the back seat.

"You told him?" I say practically hysterically.

"No, I didn't have to. My brothers aren't dumb, and as the baby, they've been looking out for me my entire life," he reminds me, and I fully understand since Saint and Shepp treat me the exact same way.

"He won't say anything,"

"I know. For now, at least because you know just like I do, no one wants to have to answer to Josh over another secret,"

"True. I swear if he learns about another secret one of us has, his head is going to explode,"

"Facts!" I agree, laughing with Jabarri.

"Alight, we'll tell them soon,"

"Thanks, baby," he says, taking my hand as the driver navigates the road to take us back to the airport. I watch the unreal scenery out of the window, thinking, Hawaii was amazing and I can't wait to come back. This island is not one of the popular ones, so it was not filled with tourists, and as an introvert, it was perfect.

It's been several weeks since we have been back from Hawaii and Jabarri has been on a strong campaign to tell everyone about us being together and engaged. We were going to tell everyone at the family dinner, but all hell broke loose when Brooklyn came heavily pregnant with Uncle Aryan's baby, and he knew she was pregnant. I swear, I think all the brothers were going to take turns beating his ass. And just when we thought things couldn't get worse, his sister-in-law shows up! I thought Brooklyn was going to go into labor. She was so understandably upset. Then, after a quick private conversation with

Brook, he came back and explained who this woman was and a past he kept from everyone, and I think all of our hearts broke from the story he told. I remember looking across the table at Jabarri when DJ realized there was yet another secret between the brothers. I had to fight back the smile that was trying to break free, remembering the conversation Barbie and I had in Hawaii.

"You're not focusing, Skai," Jabarri barks at me and he is right since I have a gun in my face.

"Jabarri, I am already proficient with a gun. I do not need all this extra training,"

"You know how to use a gun on your own, but you need to practice shooting with a partner,"

"Why?" I ask, pouting. He has been on this training kick, and I do not understand why.

"Because Aryan's late wife's sister has potentially brought trouble to our doorstep, and I want you ready to face anything that may happen,"

"Fine," I acquiesce because he has a good point. We don't know if this man is going to act a fool, and if he does, we all need to be ready.

"You need to be able to feel your partner's moves, anticipate his or her next move, have their back,"

"Okay," I say. Even though I am tired and just want to go lie down, I push through. We are back-to-back, but when I begin to focus, I feel his body, and I begin to anticipate his next moves. When he moves right, I move, I feel his weight shift, and I move backward with him. I feel his foot shift, and I move left with him. He spins, and I stay with him, my back never losing contact with his. When he begins moving across the floor, I move with him, "left," he commands, and I turn without a second thought, shooting the target's center mass. "Right," I move again. At one point, I spin in front of him, my back to his chest, and turn so we are chest to chest as I take out the targets behind him. By the time we are done, my arms are aching from all the shooting we've done, but if something goes down, I will not be the weakest link.

"You are getting too good, baby, but a word of advice. Always take the head shot. They can wear something to protect their chest but not their head."

"Okay," I say because that makes sense, especially with Kevlar. There are so many different options other than the basic bulletproof vest, but a head shot is a guaranteed kill.

"Once we get this baby shower over with, I think we should finally tell our family about us,"

"Okay," I finally give in because it's time. Honestly, it's been time, if Aryan and Brooklyn hadn't dropped bombs the night of the family dinner they would have already known.

"That was too easy. I was expecting a real fight."

"Naw, it's time, and besides, I'm ready to begin planning our wedding."

"You are going to be a stunning bride. I can't wait to see you walk down the aisle to me."

"Me too. And I can't wait to do all the wedding things with my mom."

"Yeah, Savvy is going to go all out for her only daughter."

"Yeah, probably," I say, smiling from ear to ear. "But I would love for it to be just us,"

"I mean, we can try. But even if we only do family and closest friends, it will still be a huge event."

"True. Alright, I guess it's a small price to pay to finally become your wife. I mean, you made me wait long enough," I tell him, walking past him. "Eeekkk!" I scream as he scoops me up and throws me over his shoulder.

"I kept you waiting? If it wasn't for you we probably would've been married before your mom and my brother got married. I knew who you were to me the moment I set my eyes on you."

"Jabarri," I whisper as he sets me down staring me in my eyes so I can see that he means what he is saying.

"I am just stating facts. But I am a firm believer in things happen for a reason and when they are supposed to happen. We both had to grow and mature so we could get to this place, and even though it took years just knowing we are together, I know it was worth it."

"I love you, baby,"

"I love you, too. I have to show you something, but first I need to go by your house. Okay?"

"Yeah, lets go," I tell him.

CHAPTER 12

*J*abarri

I watch her dance around the room, and I know I made the right decision. That day after our gun training I told her I wanted to show her something but I had to go by her house first. The truth is what I wanted to show her was at her house. When we got to the house I went to the room and called her asking her to come here for a second. She had an empty room downstairs she kept saying she was going to make into another sitting room so I took it upon myself to finish the room while she was at work, or away recruiting for her brother. She never even realized what was happening in her own house. When she opened the door, she skidded to stop in the doorway. "Jabarri?" her hands clamp over her mouth as her eyes travel the room taking in everything.

"Do you like it?"

"I love it." She walks around the room touching everything.

"Why didn't I think to do this?"

"Cause it was meant for me to do it for you,"

"This is a gorgeous dance studio."

"You dancing for me will always be one of my favorite memories and it looked like you really missed dancing. So, I wanted to give you your own place to dance," I tell her and she turns to me, rising on her tip toes to kiss me. I put in a wall of mirrors, a bar against a wall, a ton of lights, and a sound system that the movie theater would be jealous of. There is movable pads for her to use and even a piano. Everything she could possibly need to dance to her heart's content.

"You are amazing, you know that?"

"I mean I knew that but it's nice that you finally know it."

"Barbie, hush," she says, laughing, still going through everything.

"Were did you get these pictures from?" she asks, referring to the photo collage of her on one wall.

"I had Jassiel get them from your mom"

"Oh my God, look at these!" she says, turning to notice the giant pictures of her I have on another wall.

"I picked my favorite pictures of you dancing," I explain.

"This is too much," she says.

"It's not enough for you. All I want is to be able to watch you some of the time when you dance. I know this a private thing for you, to decompress, so I don't want to interfere too much."

"It is a personal thing for me but so are you and you can watch me anytime."

"Thank you, beautiful. Oh, and in the lockers over there are some outfits for you to wear, unless you want to dance for me in your birthday suit," I tell her, waggling my eyebrows at her. The smile that blooms across her face makes me so happy, not because I may actually get the chance to see her dance in all her naked glory, but because she was comfortable with the comment. She didn't turn away from me, or start fidgeting like she would have in the past, and I love that. I think her and I continuing to go to couples therapy has helped after the Alayna debacle and making love, we had a lot to discuss. One thing I have worked diligently to provide for her is a safe space, a safe space to emote, to talk to me about anything and not have to worry about judgement or my feelings coming into play. I will not take over, or try to fix the problem unless she wants me too, but I want to be her safe space in all things. Coming to therapy has taught me how to verbalize correctly and effectively and also how to identify what I am feeling properly and that has made me a better man, not just for her, but for myself as well. And she is getting there too, a lot slower than me, but I don't care how long it takes for her to get there. I will be there with her every step of the way.

"You know they say great minds think alike right?"

"Yeah, I say questioningly,"

"Come with me," she takes my hand, walking out of her dance studio and walking me through the house towards the garage. "I don't know how we both pulled this off without either of us noticing, maybe we were to busy trying to surprise each other,"

"Probably," I say, truly curious as we stop in front of the door that leads to the garage.

"Open it," she says moving away and when I do I was not prepared.

"Nöku Ahi," I say astonished. "How did you pull this off?" I ask.

"I know you wanted to get into this, you kept talking about it so I started planning. And this is a bit self-serving because I want to buy it from you so I can give it to my mom when you are done,"

I step in the garage and look at the 2007 Monte Carlo SS that needs a shit ton of work sitting there. Along with an impact wrench, air compressor, grinder, and toolbox that I assume is full of tools with a huge bow on it.

"Naw, I would have noticed this coming in no matter how busy I am."

"I know, that's why I had them bring it all today and I disabled the alerts and cameras on your phone,"

"I've taught you too much shit," I tell her as she walks into my arms, rising on her tiptoes to give me a kiss. Yeah, it's stuff like that that lets me know I am heading in the right direction with her. We walk into the garage, and I begin to assess the damage to the car. It's not in horrible shape, but it definitely needs a lot of work. All of my brothers have carved out hobbies for themselves, but all I had was computers, and I love what I do. I am damn good at it, but I wanted to do more. I can build a computer from a VHS player and hack into damn near anything on this planet, but at this point, it's no longer providing me a challenge. I have always loved cars. I remember when

I first met Shepp, we instantly hit it off over our love of cars. I've had the thought to try my hand at car restoration and said as much to Skai about it, and she goes and does this. Yeah, we got to hurry up and talk to Savvy and Josh; I need her as my wife now.

"You haven't taught me enough," she says provocatively, and my eyebrows touch my hairline.

"Don't bite off more than you can chew, Sprite,"

"Jabarbie, don't get fucked up! I told you about that stupid ass nickname," she says, and I burst out laughing at her. The woman is tiny, tongue sharp as a samurai sword. She is as dangerous as any of us, and her heart is as pure as they come. The. Perfect. Fucking. Woman.

"I couldn't help it,"

"Whatever," she says, preparing to walk away, but I pull her back to me. "Don't leave yet," I whisper in her ear, and she shivers in my arms. "Don't start something you aren't going to finish."

"Who said I wasn't prepared to finish it?" she turns in my arms, cupping me.

"Fucking tease," I groan, resting my forehead against hers until she wiggles out of my arms and runs back in the house, leaving me in the garage hard and needy, knowing I'll follow her. I find her pants and socks in the hallway. A few feet later, her shirt is on the floor. I turn the corner and several steps later find her panties, yeah, she's definitely a tease. Skai very seldomly wears a bra, so I know she is somewhere in this house beautifully naked. I hear music coming from her studio, and I hurry my steps, knowing she is indeed dancing naked, but when I cross the threshold, I am woefully unprepared for the sight that greets me. *Robin Thicke's Lost Without You* is playing. The lights are dim, and she is moving that sexy body to the music. Even though I am so hard it hurts, I am transfixed on the performance taking place in front of me. The way she rolls her body, her muscles flexing and relaxing, is mesmerizing, and I make a mental note to put a stripper pole in here for her because right now she'll give the best stripper a run for their money. She cups her breasts as she dances, looking at me with more heat and desire in her eyes than I have ever seen from her before. When her hand begins traveling toward her pussy, I move. I am naked with her in my arms before I can even register moving.

"Put your leg up," I instruct her as I walk her over to the mirrored wall that has the barre on it. She shows off her flexibility, easily extending her leg across the bar. "Show off. Both hands on the mirror, I want you to watch us make love, Nöku Ahi. I want you to watch us fuck." She moans at my words. "Hmm, does my baby get turned on from watching? A little voyeur in the making, huh? Would you like to go to Asher's club so you can watch someone else get fucked? Would that turn you on? Would you let me fuck you in a room full of people, Skai? Letting go, knowing I will keep you safe and that I will kill expeditiously anyone who dared touch you? Is there an inner freak in there? I can't wait to bring her out. Touch yourself," I tell her, I look in the mirror and can see her wetness coating her thighs. "That's it beautiful, make yourself feel good," I tell her gripping my dick and I watch her rub herself, undulating on her hips, chasing her orgasm. "You look so fucking sexy, baby,"

"Help me, Jabarri, I need more,"

"Oh, I got more, Skai." Leaning forward I cover one of her hands with mine as I plaster myself to her back. I use the other hand to rub the head of my dick up and down her slit, wetting it with her juices before I place the head at her opening and push inside of her.

"Jabarri," she moans out, her hand dropping from playing with herself.

"I didn't say stop," I growl out.

"Oh fuck, I can't, Jabarri."

"Yes, you can," I tell her, still holding myself at her entrance.

"Jabarri, stop teasing me and get inside of me."

"You don't tell me what to do," I tell her. She doesn't say anything but before I can take my next breath, she pushes back taking me to the hilt.

"Fuck!" I yell out completely unprepared for that. "You're greedy, baby, but that's okay I got you," I tell her, pulling out before sliding back in. I swear it feels like I'm fucking a slip and slide she's so wet. "Fuck, Nöku Ahi, this won't take long. I am not going to last long.

Look at us, baby, how beautiful we look." I cup a breast, playing with her nipple. "Keep playing with yourself, Skai,"

"Manaia, you feel so damn good, I am so close. Cum with me, baby," she says, pushing back on me. She's going to take both of us over the edge if she keeps doing what she's doing.

"Massage him, baby," I tell her, and my knees almost buckle when her internal muscles clamp down and release before repeating the action. Skai told me once that she does like a million kegels a day and I can tell, as she literally gives me an internal hand job.

"Are you close?"

"I'm ready."

"Cum with me," I tell her, pushing her hand aside and pinching her clit, hoping she cums because my orgasm is barreling down, and there is nothing I can do to stop it. She clamps down on me so hard I can barely move and we cum together. Her legs are shaking, I help her take her leg down, before I pick her up and carry her to the bedroom.

CHAPTER 13

*S*kai

Sleeping alone feels weird, but considering that today is Brooklyn's baby shower, Jabarri thought it best if he stayed home last night. I am so used to his big body giving me a heat stroke that I almost couldn't sleep last night. So, I am a tad bit cranky, but I'll pull it together by the time I get to the compound. I am not a dress girly, but I decide to wear one today. However, I bring some leggings, a tee shirt, and some sneakers for later because I know how these Gideon events turn out. One moment we're having a beautiful baby shower, and the next, it's an arm-wrestling turkey-wrangling event or something equally crazy. I slide my feet in some sandals, put on my jewelry, everything except my engagement ring, and my finger feels so bare without it, I grab my purse and head out the door. I take a quick look at his project and can actually see some progress, I wasn't sure about the gift since it was just talk on his part, I wanted to do something nice for him, something meaningful plus give him the chance to see if it is something he'd like doing. Since that day, he has managed to spend some time each day tinkering on the car. Even if he can't restore it, I'll get it towed to someone who can, but at least he had the opportunity to give it a try. I slide behind the wheel and head to the compound. It has been a little while since I spent time with my mom, Brooklyn, or the rest of the ladies, and it will be nice to get a chance to. Also, they can stop looking at me like I am broken, and I can finally get the chance to show them that I am no longer struggling either.

"There's my baby."

"Hi, Momma," I say seconds before I am pulled into my mom's arms, and I release a deep breath. My mom has been my best friend for as long as I knew what a best friend was, so it has been super hard keeping this Jabarri thing from her. There were only two other secrets I kept from her, my cousin and being bisexual. Both times, I was terrified to tell her, and both times, she reassured me that she loved me. We worked through the molestation, and she told me in no uncertain terms that I was her daughter and her love wasn't contingent on who I loved. Ugh, I love this woman, but telling her about Jabarri really has me a bit terrified and I can't figure out why. Maybe because I run the risk of losing her or Jabarri, and I don't want to lose either of them. One reason I ran from Jabarri for years is because it was just easier, easier than dealing with everything that comes with loving him. But I have learned one thing this past year is he's worth it. I just hope it doesn't cost me everything.

"Look at you wearing a dress," she says holding my at arms-length to look at me.

"Ma, you act like I have never worn a dress before."

"I know you've worn a dress before, little girl, after all, I am your mother. All I am saying is it's not your go-to outfit."

"True, but I thought I would dress more femininely today, but don't worry I brought a change of clothes," I tell her as we walk into the party space.

"This is gorgeous, I can't wait to see Brook's baby, I know she must be big as a house. I know I was when I carried Uncle Anson and Megan's baby Alexandria aka Lexi,"

"You really were, I don't know how you carried that big ass baby."

"Me either," I tell her, laughing. "But honestly it wasn't too bad until I got to my last month," I say thinking about the possibility of having a baby with Jabarri, it's something we have not yet discussed.

The entire family is here, including Brook's co-doctor, Dr. Mack, who is clearly smitten with Eliza. The entire shower is a typical Gideon event, crazy and hilarious and just what I needed, Jabarri and I have been in our own bubble, and I haven't really realized how much I have missed being with my crazy family. As soon as the guests leave, we head over to the house, and I change out of my dress immediately. Jabarri let me know as soon as he had the chance to get me alone what he wanted to do to me in my dress. I was turned on instantly. The man is a damn menace. We're sitting around in the living room, talking, laughing, and just enjoying each other. It is so nice to see Uncle Aryan and Brooklyn together and happy after the past he revealed to us. He deserved to be happy again. There was a ton of food left over from Praise and Jabarri being in the kitchen. I make my fourth or fifth plate, stuffing my face as I catch Jabarri staring at me from across the room, and I nod my head. I guess it's time to tell our family about us since everyone is here. We get ready to move when his phone chirps, getting his attention.

"Someone is coming back, probably forgot something," he says. The doorbell rings, and the next events happen in super slow motion. Liam goes to answer the door since he was coming back from the kitchen with his, I don't know, tenth plate, maybe. He swings the door open and is met with a gun. The shot hits him center mass at point-blank range, making him go flying backward with the force of the impact. He somehow manages to kick the door close before hitting the ground hard.

"Liam!" Emerson screams, running over to him when all hell breaks, loose and gunfire opens up. In a matter of seconds, everyone has a gun in their hands.

"Who the fuck is stupid enough to try to hit us at our own house?" DJ says, walking past the window as the gunfire takes out the windows to get to Savvy, who has a gun.

"We know where to go," Joseph says, but DJ says,

"No! Not with the women being here, we all stay in here, together, and we make them sorry they ever tried this shit," DJ says just as a bullet comes in from the back shattering the glass retractable wall.

"Fuck, we're surrounded," Anson says.

"We'll hold them off. You ladies go, get our stuff, and get back here ASAP," Asher says.

"Who is this? And why are they here?"

"Nabeck," Alondra says, looking out of the window.

"He couldn't have gotten this many of his men across the border," Jaasiel says.

"He probably hired these men once he got to America," Joseph says.

All the other women come back in the room looking like female *Rambos*. Liam is fine. His chest will be bruised, and he may have bruised or broken ribs, but he's alive. His new line of Kevlar made sure of it. I know he is in pain, but he finds a window and begins returning fire. Emerson takes a rifle up on a higher floor to find a nest. Jabarri hands her a communication device so we can stay in contact with her. She takes the stairs two at a time, disappearing up the stairwell. I take up position next to Brooklyn, and my mom, returning fire, too. We are killing as many as we can, but they just keep coming like roaches.

"How many did he bring?" Jabarri yells.

"I think our reputation caused him to overcompensate," Atlas yells back.

"They're making their way to the house!" Asher says.

"No matter what, they cannot get inside the house," DJ says, and I know he's right. We don't have enough people to successfully fight them off if they get inside this house.

"If they are coming for the boy, this ain't the best way. What if they kill him?" Anson says.

"I think it's a matter of if I can't have you, no one can," Mom says as she shoots, taking out two of the men approaching the house. True looks like the black version of Tomb Raider, shooting with both guns, and Parker isn't far behind.

"There are too many!" someone yells right before a loud whistle sounds out seconds before there is an explosion.

"Who was that?"

"Most likely Emerson, she is pissed about Liam."

"I can't say I blame her."

"I needed target practice, but this shit is getting old," True says, taking out another four men.

"More are getting behind us!" Eliza says.

"Hey, Asher, once we make it out of this, hurry up and get those tunnels done," DJ says.

"That will be one of the first things on my list," he says. More shots start coming from the back, and we shift into two teams, one to protect the front and the second to protect the back.

"Let's finish this," Atlas says.

"Why didn't we make the windows bulletproof again?"

"Because we never thought anyone would be so bold and stupid to try to hit us at home," I say.

"Guess the joke is on us," Asher says. Suddenly the gunfire stops.

"The movement outside has stopped, but not all of them are dead," Emerson says through the speaker.

"Maybe they are waiting on reinforcements," Jabarri says.

"Check-in!" DJ says, and everyone sounds off safe.

"Aryan," Brooklyn's voice gets my attention immediately.

"I think my water broke," Brooklyn says, standing there holding her stomach. Damn, as if this shit is crazy enough already. Aryan looks like he is going to faint. He's white as a sheet, and that's saying a lot.

"Whatever we are going to do, we better do it now. It is not going to remain quiet for long," Joseph says, and as if he conjured it the gunfire opens up.

"Aryan, get her out of here! Emerson is going to cover your exit, and Lennox is sending the medi-copter. Take her and go," Josh says.

"Come on. We will get you to the backfield," True and Atlas say, ready to escort us out.

"Can you walk, baby?" He asks her, and I can't imagine the absolute terror he is feeling right now.

"To protect my child, hell yeah!" she says, reloading her gun and stuffing a few clips in her bra before making her way to the back of the house.

"Now, Emerson," DJ says, and several explosions go off, and we head out the back as quickly and quietly as possible. We make it a good distance without issue, but just as I think we may make it, gunfire opens up.

"You guys are almost clear. We'll hold them off," Atlas says as he and True move back-to-back, arms raised together, shooting. They shoot, turn, and shoot some more in perfect unison. They are one of the deadliest couples I have ever known and I hope Jabarri and I get to be as deadly together.

Jabarri and I dance the waltz as we switch from back-to-back, side to side, making our way across the room until Jabarri's back hits the wall and my back hits his chest as we continue to unload clips. Jabarri releases his empty clip, and I catch it, pulling a fresh clip out and slamming it into his gun, and get back to shooting.

Eliza just did some type of move where she practically ran up the guy's chest before landing on his shoulder, wrapping her legs around his neck, causing him to flip and snap his neck. And that is why she is former secret service. Finally, we hear the familiar sounds of sirens as we kill the last few left in the house. We look like hell, and the main section of the house looks like a war zone, but no one is seriously hurt, and the threat has been eliminated.

"Aryan, Brooklyn, the baby?" Jaasiel asks.

"Both are fine and should be at the hospital by now. Lennox has them. I am heading to the hospital as soon as we clear this up," Aryan informs us.

Soon the living room is filled with policemen and other crime scene techs, along with the General and we spend the rest of the night explaining what happened. Lucky for us, there is video of the whole event thanks to Jabarri, and since Mississippi is a stand-your-ground state, we had every right to defend our home. We take a moment to sneak off while everyone else is busy.

"Nöku Ahi, are you okay?" he asks me, pulling to him, hugging me and patting me down at the same time.

"Manaia, I'm fine. I promise," I say seconds before he kisses me hard. "I am not sure if it is a sign that the day we were going to let our family know about us, there's a gunfight. Maybe..."

"Nope, we are doing that shit! Aryan's situation was lingering, and it had nothing to do with us that they decided tonight to die. We are going to talk to them okay, because you are going to be my wife, Skai, okay?"

"Okay," I say.

"Now get back out there. I'll use the other exit. I hope they hurry up and get this shit over with. I need to hold you."

"Me too," I say tiptoeing to kiss him. Between him not being with me last night and this bullshit, I need to feel the safety of his arms.

CHAPTER 14

*J*abarri

The house is a disaster, they came at us from all sides, but that was probably the only reason we are still alive. That is a lot of house to try to cover, even for fifty-ish men. It spread them out and allowed us to take them out in smaller groups. Had they just split into two groups and come at us, they might have stood a chance. But then again, every person in that house is a trained fighter, so either way, they were in for a fight. We have moved the entire family to the resort, but it certainly isn't the compound. We had to cancel some bookings, but Shepp allowed us to put them up at his hotel instead for the inconvenience. That night, I felt like a teenager sneaking out. We packed as much as we could and headed to the resort, but as soon as I could, I was on my way to Skai. I chose the house furthest away from my brothers so I could hopefully make moves without them being all up in my business. Truthfully, we all had our hands full with wives, children, and now the rebuilding of the compound. Asher has been working overtime to get our living situation redesigned. We had toyed with the idea of tearing it down to the ground and rebuilding, and then someone suggested, since we have so many acres, to tear down the compound and build individual homes.

When we built the compound, we did not have wives or kids in mind, so there is some merit in having individual homes instead of one big house. However, that house is as much a part of the family as the rest of us are, but we all have to agree.

But in the midst of all of the uncertainty, Aryan and Brooklyn are finally getting married. I swear my brother moved slower than molasses in winter, but he finally got his head on straight. I mean, after he confessed about his first wife and child, I understood to a point, but the other part of me wanted to punch him in the mouth. He had a woman who wanted him and loved him, and he was out here acting stupid. Meanwhile, I had to wait and fight to have Skai in my life. I double-check my tux in the mirror and head to the wedding. Skai is the Maid of Honor, and I can't wait to see her and ogle her from across the room. I like turning her on, knowing it's just me who's gonna take care of her later. I like watching her squirm, knowing she is wet and dripping, needing me to get her right. That shit turns me on. I focus back on the task at hand before I say fuck the wedding and go steal Skai and run away with her. I grab my keys and head out.

Skai

The wedding was beautiful. I was so happy to see my friend finally getting married to the man she loves. And it was equally nice to see Aryan loving on Brook open and freely. After the wedding, we danced all night long, about halfway through, I came up out of my shoes because my feet were over it by then. I also spent the entire night avoiding Jabarri's stares. He is such an asshole. He knows exactly what he does to me when he stares at me like he is. When everyone's attention is on other stuff, I sneak out of the ballroom and slip into the empty room next to it. The room is dark, only illuminated by the moonlight coming in through the glass doors. I make my way to an empty table and sit down. Our events are always entertaining, but they can sometimes get a little overwhelming. I can hear the muted music coming from the party as I lay my head on the table, closing my eyes, and release a deep breath.

"Can I have this dance?" Jabarri asks, and I am not surprised that he found me in here. I felt him as soon as he walked in, even though he was completely silent. I don't bother to lift my head off of the table. I simply roll my head to other side to look at him.

"No," I say, smiling. "My feet and body hurt." He takes a seat in front of me, leaning down to pull both of my feet in his lap, and he begins to massage to my feet.

"That feels so good," I moan.

"You look so beautiful, baby. I can't wait to see you coming down the aisle to me."

"We have to finally talk to DJ and my mom."

"We tried at the baby shower,"

"Yeah, until it was battle royale,"

"Right. And I wouldn't dare do it now. It's Aryan and Brooklyn's day."

"Yep. So where does that leave us?"

"Maybe we don't plan anything right now and just go with the flow,"

"We can just be a couple," I suggest.

"And how do you think Josh and your mother would feel about that?"

"Probably betrayed, but they might not care?" I say, looking at him, and the look on his face says be fucking for real. "Fine." I concede.

"Well, we'll just focus on us."

"Focusing on you is easy," he says as he hits a spot on my foot that makes me slide down further in my seat as I moan out my appreciation for his massage.

"You better cut that out before we see how steady this table really is."

"Well, wouldn't that be a way to let our family know we're together? Hearing us fucking in the next room."

"Yeah, I like being able to breathe without assistance, so I'll control myself,"

"Yeah, and even though I am grown, my momma will still knock the hell out of me. I can hear her now, *'You're not that grown, little girl!'*"

"That definitely sounds like Savvy," he says, laughing. "Hey, what are you doing?" he asks when I pull my feet back from his lap.

"One of us better get back to the party,"

"You," he says.

"Why me?"

"Oh, cause I told them I was leaving, so they'll be looking for you, not me."

"Damn, I should've thought of that."

"Well, go say your goodbyes, and I will meet you in the parking lot. Let's go home," he suggests, helping me stand and walking me to the door. I turn left, and he goes straight to the front of the hotel. I make my way into the ballroom and head directly to my mom.

"Hey, Sweetness, are you okay?"

"Hi, Momma, I'm fine, just tired. I am going to head home."

"Do you need someone to drive you home?"

"No, Ma, I don't want anyone to have to leave the party just to take me home. I'll be fine."

"Are you sure?"

"Yes,"

"Okay, how about a spa day? Just you and me?"

"Oouu! Yes, please," I say, grinning from ear to ear.

"Okay, I'll make the reservation. Text me when you get home."

"Okay," I tell her, hugging her tight. "Tell DJ good night for me."

"I will," she says. I make my rounds, saying good night before heading to get my car, and just like he said he would, he was waiting for me and we head home.

It is our first game of the season, and Saint has stacked his team with pure talent, but the other team doesn't stand a chance. I'll be on the sidelines with him, and the entire family is coming to support Saint and the team. We had custom sweatsuits made for the coaches and staff. I, of course, had to get something different because I am so much smaller than everyone else. So instead of wearing a sweatsuit, I wear a jumpsuit with *The Hut* on the back with my sneakers and sun visor cause Mississippi heat will have you on a three hundred degree slow roast. It's time for the team to take the field. They are lined up in the tunnel with Saint up front so he can run out with his team. The stadium is a sea of navy blue with navy blue and gold shaker poms screaming as they wait for the team to take the field. Saint has worked hard since he came here to build an amazing football team and bring school spirit and pride back to the college. It has gone from an okay school to one of the most desired schools to attend and the crowd is proof of that. The music changes, and you can feel the energy in the stadium change. I swear it's electric. When *Swag Surfin* by *F. L. Y.* comes on, the roar shakes the stadium, and the team runs out on the field as the band, cheerleaders, and majorettes flank them on either side. I am at the back,

"Good luck, baby," Jabarri says, making me turn around.

"Thanks, baby," I say. He sticks his hand out, and we slap the back of our hands before double slapping palms, locking thumbs as we come in for a hug, and then sliding our hands apart with a snap at the end. I turn and run out on the field, and all you see is blue swaying from side to side. The team is in a huddle chanting, *The what? The Hut! The what? The Hut! That's right!* They are hype and ready to win this game, and I almost feel bad for the other team, but I don't because they've been talking way too much shit for me to care about the ass-whipping they are about to get. The family is taking up the first several rows, ready to enjoy the game. We get the ball first, and it's game on.

"We didn't have to beat them that bad," Saint says after the game, it's just him and I walking out of the locker room.

"Yeah, we did. Now maybe they'll learn to keep their damn mouths shut."

"I hear you, but damn, forty-two to three is embarrassing.

"They'll be okay. Let's go, our family is waiting for us," I say and sure enough, everyone is waiting for us in the parking lot, ready to go celebrate.

CHAPTER 15

*J*abarri
"It's time," I say to Skai as she flits around her bedroom, hanging up her clothes.

"We're ready to try again?" she asks, pausing her steps to look at me. I offered to hang her clothes up so she could sit down, and she told me unequivocally no. *"You're not about to mess up my clothes handling them like I have seen you handle your clothes."* So I took a seat on the bed.

"One thing the shootout should have shown us is that life is short. I am ready to be married, baby, aren't you?" She doesn't say anything, just disappears in her closet. "Skai?" I call out to her when she doesn't immediately come back out, and when she doesn't answer I am in motion. I find her standing in front of the rack holding the shirt she went to hang up, twisting the fabric in between her fingers until the tips are white from blood loss. Reaching out, I gently loosen the fabric from around her fingers before taking the shirt to hang it up. "Talk to me," I tell her, pulling her into my arms and sinking us both to the floor. I put my back against the wall and put her back to my chest in the hopes of making it easier for her to talk if she is not looking me in my face, even though I really want to see her as she talks.

"It's just thinking of being a wife. It terrifies me at times. I want to get married one time, Jabarri, and I want to be a good wife to a good husband. I have come into this relationship with a lot of baggage,"

"And we've dealt with it,"

"We have, but how long are you going to be patient if something resurfaces?"

"So why did you say yes, Skai? Did you just say yes because you were hoping our family wouldn't support us?"

"I said yes because I want to be married, Jabarri, I just said that, didn't I? And I never really thought our family would not support us, but I knew our situation would have us taking our time telling them, and that would give me some time to work on my shit."

"Baby, I would never put my hands on you ever unless you are begging me to spank you when I have you face down and ass up," I say, and she laughs, breaking her tension just like I hoped it would. "But right now, I am very tempted to put you over my knee and give you that spanking."

"Only if you want to lose the knee you put me over and the hands you use to try to spank me,"

"So damn bloodthirsty,"

"No more than you are. I know you don't get, it but I do. I want to come to you whole, Jabarri. We've both waited a long time to get here with each other, and for years I have fought against my attraction to you. I want to be whole and present in this relationship, especially in our marriage. I do not want to be the broken woman you have to tiptoe around because you may trigger me, and I have a meltdown. This relationship shouldn't be one-sided, Barbie, and if I am not whole it will be. So yes, I want to be your wife, that's why I said yes, but I also want to be mentally healthy when we get married."

"I love you for thinking about me and our marriage like that, Nöku Ahi. Why can't you continue to work on it as my wife? I can support you, because whether we are legally married or not, you are my wife, not future wife, but my damn wife right now, and I am your husband. I am not going anywhere, no matter what. And by the way, so far, you have been an exceptional wife,"

"I'm your wife?"

"That's right."

"Then why am I still paying all my bills?" she asks and I pick her up and turn her around so fast she shrieks out a scream.

"What bills do you still pay, Skai?"

"I just paid my credit card bill today!"

"You are a complete sneaker head, Skai. How much was the last pair of sneakers you bought?"

"That is beside the point,"

"Hmm, okay, and besides that, what other bill are you paying?"

"I just paid for my own gas,"

"You paid for gas? I distinctly remember taking your car and filling it up, so when did you pay for gas Skai?"

"Almost a year ago."

"Wow."

"The point is, as your wife, I shouldn't have to pay for anything."

"I see. Where is the money coming from that you pay for all of these imaginary bills with?"

"My bank account,"

"The one ending in 6702?"

"Yep, that's the one."

"Hmm, that's the same account I deposit money in every month, so I gotta ask what bills are you paying?"

"Never mind you are completely missing the point."

"Yeah, you're right baby, I'll do better, okay?"

"That's all I am asking!"

"Right. Skai,"

"Okay. When do you want to do this?"

"Josh and Savvy will be coming back tomorrow night, and we're having a family dinner, so I think today is the best time,"

"Jabarri, it will be a pretty raw time for my mom seeing as she is moving my brothers remains here,"

"We're talking to them tomorrow night, Skai."

"Fine," she's say, giving up the fight. "Truth of the matter is my brother's body has been here and reburied. DJ took my mom away for a couple of days to give her time, so realistically there is nothing stopping us from having this conversation." She says, finally giving in. I stand with her in my arms and carry her to the bed dropping her on it.

"Let's get some sleep, we're going to have a hell of a day tomorrow.

Present Day

Skai

I sit there watching my mom spazz out, literally. DJ tries to calm her down, but she is not having it. "I lost one child, Joshua! I will not lose another one!" she tells him when he tells her to calm down. She continues to pace the room, vacillating between being pissed and being terrified.

"Mom, please calm down. I am fine, and Jabarri is running facial recognition on them, plus we killed them, so please relax for a second," My eyes track her until she finally sits down next to me, pulling me to her like I am three years old instead of a woman in her thirties and I let her.

"Skai, run through this again," DJ says, and I do. When I tried the first time, I was a little shaken up, but now that the adrenaline has tapered off, I can think a bit more clearly.

"Let's see the video," he says, and I pull out my phone to play it. I cast the video to the big TV, and we all watch the video. Jabarri made sure to remove my video portion of the video, and we all watched as the guy with the gun shot and killed the other guy, as the other guys there picked up the body and threw it in the water seconds before noticing me.

"We have a problem," Jabarri says, walking into the house. We are still at the resort since the compound is still under construction.

"There were four guys there, but there were seven men that were killed, and if that isn't bad enough, two of the original four weren't among the dead."

"So two men got away that know Skai was there, but they were able to make some calls about the situation enough so that backup came to assist," DJ summarizes.

"Well, as far as we know, they don't have a video of Skai, so they don't know who she is." Aryan says.

"Yeah, but how long is that going to last? We know they were able to make at least one phone call and get help within minutes, so how do we know they didn't get a picture of her license plate numbers?" Joseph says.

"And for all we know, they didn't get a picture of her plates, and they have no idea who she is," Jaasiel chimes in.

"You know our motto, we think and prepare for the worst but hope for the best."

"Why does his ass look so fucking familiar," Atlas asks, looking at the guy with the gun.

"Because that is Arturo, or as he is better known, Art. He worked for my father, and if I can recall, was just as ruthless and brutal, but he was a small fish," True says.

"He doesn't seem all that small right now."

"It's been eight-ish years since we six-footed Victor, that's plenty of time for someone to climb the ladder and take over the organization," True says, studying the image of the guy on the screen.

"So where does that leave us?" Anson asks.

"Skai, you'll move in with us so we can keep you safe, and we'll keep someone with you at all times," DJ says.

"No," I say immediately.

"Skai, it wasn't a question."

"Ma, I am fine. I am not moving in here,"

"Listen, menace, I agree with Savvy and Josh. Your safety is top priority."

"I appreciate that, but I am safe," I say, cutting my eye at Jabarri and can tell he wants to speak up.

"Oh yeah, how do you figure, what's going to happen if they come for you in the middle of the night? Please, Sweets, give your mother a little peace of mind and move in and let us protect you until we can figure out if they know who you are and come for you."

"Ma," I start again and it turns into a full-fledged argument between me and everyone except Jabarri. Even the wives take their husbands side and feel like I should move in with my mom and DJ.

"I am not doing it!" I yell, making everyone shut up. The idea of being away from Jabarri for just one night makes me physically ill.

"Skai Nalani Errington! You need to think about this, if you go home, you are all alone all the way across town, at least twenty minutes away. Everyone has a wife or a wife and a kid or kids. They can't be sleeping on the sofa to protect you. So what are you going to do? Who is going to protect you if you are not here?" She asks, and I release a deep breath dropping my shoulders in defeat before looking at Jabarri.

"I will," he says, dropping the bomb in the middle of the room, and a blanket of silence falls over the room.

CHAPTER 16

*S*kai

      This is not how it was supposed to go, and I am physically ill to my stomach. We were supposed to have a one-on-one conversation with my mom and DJ, but they kept pushing about me moving in with them and wouldn't take no for an answer. Jabarri has been trying to get me to tell our family for months, and I kept dragging my feet, but now I wish I had. Oh well, it's too late to change anything now. Jabarri walks over, pulling me in his arms, finally getting the hug I know he wanted to give me before, making me melt into him.

"Well, I'll be damned," Jaasiel says.

"In here, NOW!" DJ says to me and Jabarri. I look at him and my mom to try and gauge their feelings, but they both have their faces set on neutral. *Shit.* I think. This is a cluster fuck. I disentangle myself from him, but he grabs my hand, giving it a little squeeze in support as we walk to the back room with them.

"How long has this been going on, Skai?" my mom asks, obviously hurt by the fact that I kept this a secret from her. This is one of the only secrets I have ever kept from her, and I feel like shit keeping this from her. When Jabarri continued to push to tell our family, I fought against it, but I did not think of the ramifications. I didn't think about the look my mom would have when she found out I kept this a secret from her, the look that I am looking at right now, and all I want to do is cry. Goodness, how did I fuck this up so badly?

"Umm," I hedge, biting my bottom lip.

"Spit it out, Skai,"

"Well, uh, it's been a year," I say so low it's barely audible but my mom hears like a bat, so I am sure she heard me.

"A year!? You kept this a secret from me for a whole year?"

"Yes," I once again whisper out.

"And Jabarri, what about Natalie?" DJ asks.

"If you could just sit down, we can explain," Jabarri says, and luckily for us, they do, and we tell them how the past year went and Natalie's secret.

"And you decided to keep this a secret? Why?" my mom asks.

"I wasn't sure how y'all would feel, Ma. Technically, he's my uncle, and we weren't sure how you guys would feel. We didn't want to take the risk of losing our family if you and DJ were against this, even if everyone else was okay."

"Hmm," my mom says, looking over to DJ as he holds her hand. Jabarri rubs my back as we sit on the sofa across from them. No one is saying anything.

"Ma, please tell me you are not mad at me, that you understand, please."

"But I don't understand, Sweets. You are my child, my daughter. How could you misjudge your mother so badly, twice now? You kept your sexuality a secret, you kept what happened with your cousin a secret, and now this. How could you think that I would turn my back on you or not support you?" she asks, and I know she has told DJ about my past because she asked me if I would be okay with her telling him and I said yes. I also know that she knows if I am with a man, well with Jabarri, that I told him about my past too.

"Ma," I try.

"No, hush and listen. Jag and I knew for years that Jabarri was in love with you and truth be told you loved him too, but you weren't ready to admit it. We were waiting on the two of you to come to us. We also knew that things had changed between you too, but I don't think we thought things had gotten this far between the two of you,"

"You knew?" I almost screech.

"We knew," DJ says, and I wanted to kick my own ass for allowing fear to keep secrets from my mother.

"Well, damn," Jabarri says.

"And what do you feel about us, Momma?" I asked because her opinion and feelings about this means everything to me.

"How do I feel?" she asks, and I shake my head. She looks over to DJ who has been pretty quiet for the most part, then back to me. "It's about time." she says and I take my first real breath.

"Jabarri," DJ calls him.

"Yeah?"

"That is my wife's daughter, and for all intents and purposes, my daughter. If you're not about to step up and do right, leave this shit alone now."

"We're engaged," he drops yet another bomb, and I drop my head in exasperation.

"Jabarri," I say almost exhausted from his bomb dropping today.

"That's good because if you hurt her, lie to her, betray her trust, not be gentle with her, or don't love her right....she'll be a widow. Mohio?"

"Understood," Jabarri says and DJ nods at him, but the look he's leveling on him says try me.

"Savvy?"

"Yeah?"

"I have been wanting to ask you this for a while now, but I couldn't figure out how I could without tipping y'all off but, uh, where is her cousin?"

"Jabarri," I try but he just grabs my other hand, holding it never taking his eyes from my mom.

She looks over to DJ, who gives her a slight nod. "Skai only asked once and never asked again and I gave her a generic answer, but she is old enough and healed enough to know. He's dead."

"Ma, he's dead?"

"Graveyard dead. Your father and I went to talk to him. We were going to press charges on him, and we walked in on him doing the same thing to another cousin that was even younger than Skai. He lied and tried to blame it on her, but when that didn't work, he bolted, running from the house, and he stayed hidden for a while. One day, I was on lunch and spotted him. He was living in a studio in a not-so-good part of town. We went in that night, and let's just say he'll never be found."

"Ma," I whisper out because for all of these years, I lowkey felt like my mom didn't do anything about what happened to me, but she literally killed him.

"I didn't tell you because I didn't want you feeling guilty about it, one, me taking someone's life and, two, someone's life being taken because of what he did to you. I didn't want you living with all that guilt. I know you felt like I swept it under the rug, but I promise you I didn't. You are my child and I didn't feel one moment of regret or grief over it. There isn't anything I wouldn't do for you, your brothers, or my grands," she says, and I am off the sofa and in her arms in seconds, crying.

"Well, that explains why I couldn't find him," I hear Jabarri say to DJ. "Knowing Savvy, I should have known."

"I love you, Mom."

"I love you too, baby. Now let's talk about how we plan to keep you safe."

"She's with me pretty much all of the time."

"But there are going to be times when she can't be with you,"

"True, so we'll coordinate someone else being with her, and I will begin digging to try and find who is gonna end up dead. I just got you, baby, and I refuse to lose you to anyone," Jabarri says, hugging me when I pull back from his kiss.

"Not in front of my momma," I tell him, looking at him like he is crazy.

"Really, Skai?" he asks.

"If you want us both to live long enough to get married, you better act with some decorum in front of my mother," I tell him.

"Well, if we are going to set up a schedule to protect you, I suggest we go back out front so everyone can help figure this out around everyone's schedule," DJ says as he pulls me in for a hug that has Jabarri pulling me out of.

"Watch it!" he snaps at DJ, making him laugh. As soon as we walk back in the room we hear,

"It's about damn time. Now that y'all have figured that out can we please get down to business?" Atlas asks. *That's my Uncle Atty*, I think.

We sit around for the next hour or so making a preliminary schedule, and I am grateful the women aren't here, but I know they already know what's going on not only because they don't keep secrets from each other but mainly because, quiet as it's kept, the men are huge gossips. When my phone chirps and I see the two-word text from Brooklyn, I know I am right. It simply says, *lunch tomorrow!* I don't need the time or location I already know when and where to go. I reply with a simple, *ok*. Ugh, I am not prepared for the Spanish Inquisition I know is coming tomorrow.

CHAPTER 17

Skai

"Bitch! Be so for real right now! I don't know if I need to be hurt or happy for you?" Brook says as soon as I sit down at the table. All the wives are there, including True who was there yesterday so she already knew what was going on.

"I'm sorry, Brook,"

"It all makes sense now, what you said at Lennox's party and all the other stuff."

"You don't know how bad I wanted to tell you. How many times I could have used your advice,"

"Why didn't you?" she asks, and I can hear the genuine hurt in her voice.

"Because you would have told Aryan, and he would have told his brothers, and then my momma would've been on my ass."

"How did she take it?" Parker asks.

"She was not the least bit surprised. She was hurt that I kept it a secret from her. But she's okay now,"

"Well, I am surprised and, nosey so let's hear it, and I want all the details!" Megan says.

"I have no idea how your ass could be surprised, Ms. I've been married for years and kept it a secret," True says.

"That's rich coming from the woman who kept her daddy, and the shit her and her man was up to a secret,"

"Hmm, touche," True says with a shrug. I will soon be a sister too, not just a friend to them, so much is going to change but remain the same at the same time.

"Wait! Is that an engagement ring?" Brooklyn butts in, and I blush so hard it was answer enough. "Oh, naw, we need answers, and we need them now. How did y'all get engaged without us? We didn't get a chance to give you a party or nothing! This is bullshit."

"Brooklyn," I try but she is genuinely hurt, and I know I have to make this up to her. I tell them a brief rundown of what went down between Jabarri and me.

"So wait, Natalie is a lesbian?"

"Yes,"

"So Jabarri was basically her beard?"

"Yep, apparently, her parents are weird and controlling as hell, and Jabarri was the only way she could get any real freedom."

"I mean, that's obvious. What parent buys houses for their children right next door?"

"Right, most parents be ready to get rid of their kids," Joyce says.

"Naw that was your weird ass momma," True says. "But regular parents understand that their kids will eventually start living their own lives and eventually accept it."

"Well, she's come out to her parents and is currently living with her girlfriend. Her brother left the country," I say.

"Damn, you know it's serious when you feel like you have to leave an entire country to get away from your parents," Megan says and we all agree.

"Well all I want to know is how was it being with a man for you?" Carla asks.

"It was definitely different but Jabarri took his time with me, so I felt safe and loved. Being in Hawaii behind a waterfall helped with the ambiance, too."

"Hawaii," Joyce says.

"A waterfall?" Parker asks.

"Yep,"

"Them damn Gideons! They know what they be doing. What man can live up to over-the-top shit they do for us? The do the shit, get you hooked and spoiled, knowing you'll end up lost and turned out over their asses," Brooklyn says. And each one of us nods because she is right.

"The good thing is they keep it up. They will consistently put their money where their mouths are," True says.

"True," we all agree.

"Well, I would like to give you an engagement party," Brooklyn tells me.

"I'm okay with that. It has been so long and so hard keeping the engagement a secret, now I can finally act like a soon-to-be bride. But first, we have to give Ms. Parker over here a baby shower! Ma'am, that baby is gonna be huge," I say, referring to the stomach that seems to have appeared overnight.

"Listen, first of all, I am too old for this shit! Secondly, this baby has completely rearranged my internal organs, I swear he be in there using my kidneys as stress balls!"

"He? You're having a boy?!" we all ask.

"Brooklyn hasn't done an ultrasound to determine the gender but I feel like this big headed baby is a boy," she explains and you can see all our hopes deflate.

"Well let's get to planning, we have two huge celebrations to put together," Brooklyn says and we spend the next several hours planning Parker's baby shower but I was told I could not participate in the planning of my bridal shower. Since the house was destroyed and is beginning construction, we decided to have a destination baby shower and engagement party. I was at least informed it wouldn't be here. They didn't want to do too much planning where I was concerned until they got with my mom and Momma B. I feel the weight I have been carrying around lift now that everything was out in the open. I also talked to the women about the shootout, and of course True had several guns and clips on her and even a few grenades. The woman really is a one-woman killing machine, and I love that. It is amazing how the men have come into each of our lives and have cultivated the ground with each of us that gave us the freedom to be the women we have always wanted to be without judgment or repercussions. Only a man who truly loves a woman could be okay with the level of unhinged True is and not only be okay with it but love it, foster it, and participate in it. But it isn't just Uncle Atlas, it's all of them. I look around the table at my aunts and sisters and feel a contentment I didn't even realize existed. I need this, I needed them.

Jabarri

"So, did Josh threaten to kill you," Jaasiel asks.

"Yep," I reply. "And I believe him, she is his stepdaughter so hurting her would hurt Savvy and we all know that man is crazier now about her than he was before."

"Yeah," we all say.

"But she's worth it," I say and we all agree again each of referring to our own woman.

"You waited a long time for Skai, Jabby. How does it feel to finally have the woman you have loved for almost a decade?" Atlas asks.

"Pretty damn good," I say, grinning. "But I know I had a lot of growing to do. Skai was the first thing in my life that I wanted, and I couldn't just have. I have always just asked for something and got it or set my mind to something and mastered it. Skai wasn't easy at all, she wasn't easy to get, wasn't easy to figure out, she wasn't even easy to pursue, but it built character in me and patience. Made me dig deeper than the shallow level I always operated in, and when I was finally ready, I was truly ready to go after her." I say to my brothers, talking to them in a way I couldn't talk to anyone else. We are upstairs in Bree's club while the women are in Asher's restaurant. Our protection detail will be in effect until we find out if Skai is in danger.

"Well now, that the Dr. Phil session is over can we talk about how we are going to eliminate this new threat?" Atlas says. "We have kids to consider keeping safe now and our wives, although I am not sure how much protection they actually need."

"We have trained them to handle almost any situation they could possibly run into. I mean, look at how Skai handled that car and shooting while calling for help. I couldn't be prouder," Joseph says.

"I was definitely impressed and grateful. Can you imagine how Savvy would've handled losing another child, not to mention Josh and the rest of us. Then we would have lost a brother because I don't think you would have survived losing her," Asher surmises.

"I mean, how would any of us respond?" Anson asks.

"Well, you destroyed an entire island over Megan and she didn't die. I think the satellite photo saw a single blade of grass finally growing," Aryan tells us.

"And would do it again," Anson says with absolutely no remorse.

"I have the computer cleaning up the video, she didn't intentionally video them, so the quality isn't that great or clear. It is going to take a second to clean up the image, and then I can see who all was out there with Art. If that is really Art in the first place, True said he was a low man on the totem pole, and it has been twenty years or more since she last saw him."

"Well, put a rush on that shit," Jaasiel implores.

"Trust me, I am. I don't like her potentially being in danger from an unknown threat,"

"We'll get it figured out, and handle whoever it is," Joseph says, and I have no doubt about it. My only question is how long it will take.

CHAPTER 18

kai

I sit with my legs dangling in the beautiful blue water of the Florida Keys. Parker wanted to go further, but Brooklyn asked her if she was crazy and to keep her super pregnant ass in the US. It is gorgeous here and peaceful, and we are about to disturb all of that with baby shower shenanigans. They have been in the water all day with the kids, of course, Joseph is teaching the kids swimming, diving, and holding their breaths for extended periods of time. I snuck off to have a few minutes to myself. I have been surrounded twenty-four hours a day. If I am not with Jabarri, I am with another member of the family. I love the fact that they want to protect me, but not having any privacy or time to myself has me ready to crawl out of my own skin. I am more than positive that even though I am alone right now, if I am gone too long someone will be coming to get me. The only way I was able to get away in the first place was because Momma B has them busy and snuck me out while she had the brothers running around to do her bidding. Honestly, I know without a shadow of a doubt that Jabarri knew the moment I was no longer in the villa. But truthfully, things have been completely quiet, no calls, no one following me no strangers popping up out of nowhere. Jabarri identified the shooter in the video, and Uncle Atlas asked his old contact, Doone, to see what he could dig up on Art. Jabarri found everything there was to find on paper, but Doone has other ways to find out information that leaves no paper trail, so now we're waiting to hear what he found out, if anything. I think if they were coming for me, that would have already, they probably can't figure out who I am. It wasn't like they saw my face. *Then why haven't you relaxed since that day?* My inner voice says, and she's right, but I tell her to *shut up!* There has been a perpetual knot in my stomach since that day, and it won't go away.

"Baby?" Jabarri says. I felt him before he said a word to me. For a man as big as he is, he was completely silent while walking up to me.

"Yes,"

"Do you need more time?" he asks and I grab my *Sig Sauer P365 Rose* up from my lap, tuck it in my waist holster as I stand, turning to face him. "No," I can go back. Taking my hand, he leads me back to the hotel. We walk in silence both of us enjoying our time together here in paradise. Clear blue water reflecting a clear blue sky and perfect weather. Everything is perfect.

"Are you changing for the shower?"

"I guess I better," I say, looking down at my jeans that I have rolled up midcalf, basic tee shirt, and flip flops. He leads us down the back hallway. Once we are back to the villa, we snag the downstairs bedroom that is off by itself. Whoever designed the villas had privacy in mind. The four bedrooms are far away from each other, giving the guests privacy when they need it, but the large kitchen, dining area, and living room are enough space to host large gatherings. As soon as the doors are closed, I begin stripping as I make my way to the shower, and before I know it, I am up off my feet and in Jabarri's arms.

"We'll be late," I halfheartedly protest.

"So it's not our baby shower, they'll be fine," he says, sitting me back on my feet, turning me to face him. "You're beautiful, baby. You have been stressed, let me help you with that," he says, gripping my braids, pulling my head back as he kisses me, and I am moaning in his mouth. The bathroom and baby shower all but forgotten. "I have been gentle with you, baby, I wanted you to get used to being with me, being with a man, but I think it's time to introduce you to all of me. Can you handle me, baby? Are you ready to take me fucking you like I have been wanting to since I saw you more than eight years ago?"

"Jabarri," I moan, turned on but still a little unsure. I know he won't hurt me, and I know he would stop at the first sign of discomfort from me. "Yes," I say, taking his hand and putting on my pussy.

"First, I am going to take the edge off of us both, then we are going to shower, and I am going to indulge in that mouth-watering pussy that's tucked between those sexy thighs," his finger slips easily between my lips, and he begins exploring my nubbin. "This pussy is tight, hot, wet, and ready to get fucked," he tells me as his other hand takes my hand and places it on his dick. I know immediately what to do, and I stroke him exactly like I know he likes it. He is hard and warm in my hand like heated velvet steel. I let out a startled yelp when he picks me up, carrying me to the bed as he lays down with me in his arms still. He kissed me as he slowly pushed inside of me.

"You're so big, so fucking deep." I tell him, ripping my mouth from his. "Don't stop," I tell him as he rocks inside of me slow, hard, and deep.

"I won't, baby," I claw his back when he hits a spot inside of me, pushing me to the brink so fast I am almost light-headed. Leaning over me, he damn near takes my entire breast in his mouth, making my back bow off of the bed.

"Fuck, Jabarri,"

"Hush baby, before our mommas come in here. I didn't lock the door," he tells me before taking my mouth in a hot kiss and pushes me even closer to cumming. I can feel every ridge of his dick as it drags in and out of my channel, hitting every single nerve ending I have. I wrap my legs around his back and begin pushing myself up to meet his downward strokes. My eyes cross from the pleasure. Even though he never fails to please me, I know he is holding back. It took a while to get completely comfortable with Jabarri, not just sexually but mentally and physically. Him being in my space, how I communicate with him, and how he handles me in all aspects. When I was with

Alayna, we were on equal footing, same size, same sex, some things we just understood because it was a woman issue, like cramps. I didn't have to convince her of how bad the pain was or worry that she would think I am doing too much when I asked for certain things during that time. It has taken a while to get there with him. There are things that I have to explain to him that were just understood previously, but we have found a good rhythm with each other and to his credit, he has never made me feel needy, or dramatic at all no matter what. But this sex thing is a hurdle we have struggled to overcome. He is careful with me, and I get it. My first sexual experience with a boy was beyond traumatizing, and each subsequent experience was subpar at best. And it didn't help that I freaked out on him one night when he initiated sex, and I had a complete meltdown on him. It took him hours to get to me. I was right back at my grandmother's house with my cousin. We talked about it in therapy, but ever since then, he tiptoes in the bedroom, and I have heard the stories from all the wives, except my mom, because, yuck, and I know it gets way more intense than what he and I do, but I don't know how to change it.

I barely get a few strokes before he reaches back to unhook my ankles from his back, "Put your arms around my neck," he says before placing my legs in the crook of his arms, sliding his hands up to the middle of my back and lifting. He sits back on his heels as he uses me like a fleshlight, lifting me and dropping me on his dick, and I know I am going to let this whole house know he is in here putting in work. I drive my hands in his hair so hard I scrap his scalp as I grab two handfuls of hair and hold on. "That's it, Nöku Ahi, ride me, take this dick. I want to feel you dripping off my balls onto the sheets,"

"Oh gawd," I groan into his mouth when he crushes my lips with his, exploring my mouth, biting my lip hard.

"Hurry up and cum, so I can drench you with my cum. I want to know a part of me is inside of you as you are at the party. I want your panties drenched from the combination of our cum. Every time you walk, and you feel the wetness drip out of you, it was me and only me who's dripping from you," he is whispering in my ear, and the images he is putting in my head are making me even more turned on. "There it is, you're sucking on my dick. You're nasty as fuck, you like me telling you how I am going to fuck you later after the party. How I am going to eat your pussy until you beg me to stop, until you spray your cum everywhere, and then I am going to fuck you on every surface I can get you on. And when I am ready to cum, I am going to put you on your knees so you can swallow. Every. Fucking. Drop," he says, and that's it. He slams me down, and he pushes up, and I explode. I pull his hair so hard I may have pulled some out. I throw my head back to scream but bite my lip instead to attempt to keep the sounds from spilling out.

"You are fucking gorgeous when you cum, Nalani," he says slowing down, and I realize that while I was cumming he came with me.

"We don't have time for a part two after our shower,"

"No, we don't. I'll make that up to you later on tonight."

"I bet you will," I tell him before melting into him. My head on his shoulder as I struggle to catch my breath. Carefully, he unfolds his legs, scoots off the bed, and carries me into the bathroom, turning on the shower and walking us under the hot spray. He washes both of us while he is still inside of me. Finally, he lifts me off of him and sets off a minefield of mini orgasms as he slides out of me. He waits for me to steady myself on my feet before he lets go of me, and I practically give myself a stroke as I wash my sensitive flesh. The amount of baby orgasms I have should be studied, because it can't be normal. We rush through the rest of the shower and get dressed, and we are still late when we get to the party. I want a hole to open up in the floor when the knowing looks are leveled our way. However, Jabarri didn't seem to have a problem or care. He took me by my hand and walked in the room with his chest stuck out, proud of our lateness. *Someone kill me now.*

JABARRI

I went too far with her, I let the tight control I have when I'm with Skai slip. I was rougher with her than I have ever been, and even my talk was more aggressive than I have ever been, but she didn't freak out or pull away from it or me, so that's a good sign right? God, I hope so. So far, the baby shower has been a subdued event compared to our normal parties, but we are missing part of the gang, Eliza, Emerson, Luke, Liam, and Lucas, along with Savvy's other kids, aren't present. T'Aundrea, Angie, and Dr. Mack are also not in attendance so it turned out to be basically just the immediate family along with Parker's parents. Parker is glowing and huge, and it reminds me of when Skai carried Megan and Anson's baby. I look over to her looking relaxed and happy, and I know one day she will be just as big and beautiful when she carries our babies. I wonder how many kids she would want. I know she will probably cuss me out everyday of her pregnancy, and I am looking forward to it.

"Look at her," Jassiel says, walking up to me and interrupting my mental thoughts.

"What am I looking at?" I ask, looking at him instead of her.

"I'm going to be a daddy. I had accepted the idea of never having any children. After losing a baby and never getting pregnant again, she assumed she couldn't have any more children, and I was okay with that. I have nieces and nephews and a goddaughter. When she came home and told me, I was literally light-headed. She picked up a meal from Hedonism that Praise cooked and set the table with flowers and candles. I came home pleasantly surprised. I hurried up and washed up, came back to the table when she told me she had something cooking in the kitchen. When I got in there, the oven was on, and there was bread inside warming. I didn't think anything of it, so I took it out of the oven, put it on a plate, and carried it into the dining room. I sat down to eat, not catching on at all until she said,

"What was that, Jaasiel?"

"What? The bread?" I asked.

"Yes,"

"A bun," I told her, eating, impressed with Praise's skills. She waited a few minutes longer and then asked.

"Where was it?" she asked me, and I answered on autopilot.

"In the oven," I ate several more forkfuls of food before my brain cells actually put two and two together. My fork clattered to the plate as I looked up at her, shocked but needing to verify what I thought she was saying.

"A bun in the oven!? You're pregnant? Parker!" I call her when she doesn't immediately reply. "Are you pregnant?"

"Yes, I am already in my second trimester,"

"Wait, what? So you were pregnant during that gunfight?"

"It would appear that way,"

"I wish I could dig those fuckers up so I could kill them again,"

"Your son and I are just fine. He is built Gideon tough, but I will be glad when he gives me my body back," I made my way around the table to hug her and told her I love her. Look at her now, over there glowing, big, and happy. I wonder how fast she'll let me knock her up again.

"You really need help," I look at him with my head crooked like he is crazy.

"Oh and you haven't thought about getting Skai pregnant. How she would look carrying your baby?"

She's carrying my babies inside of her right now. I think, remembering all the cum I shot inside of her earlier. "We've had other things on our minds," I tell him instead, never really answering his question. True gets our attention before he can come back to push further.

CHAPTER 19

*J*abarri

"Okay, we have a few games to play, and I am going to say right now there will be no cheating," True announces, looking directly at us. "Today is going to be the women against the men, and let the best woman win. The guys will go first, and then we will go last, and the parents will judge so it can remain fair. "First up, is the sock game, whoever can make the most matches out of this pile will be the winner. You have sixty seconds, so whoever is playing, line up," she tells everyone, and we line up, seeing as we are the only men besides Parker's dad and my dad. We are too competitive to not play every game they have today because we have to shit talk. "Alright, sixty seconds on the clock! Ready, Set, Go!" she yells, and we're off. It literally looks like a tornado swept over the table. Socks are flying everywhere.

"Why are they so fucking small?" Atlas yells as he struggles to make one match. Meanwhile, the fathers are putting matches together better than a relationship coach. And then it happens Atlas and Jospeh pick up the same sock, and neither will release it, so it becomes a wrestling match over a sock.

"Give me the damn sock! I grabbed it first!"

"The hell you did! It's my sock. You don't even have this sock in your pile!" Joseph yells. They pull on the sock until it rips, which pisses Joseph off so badly he reaches over the table and scoops up the small pile of socks Atlas has accumulated throwing them across the room, which prompts Atlas to flip the entire table, making everyone's socks go flying.

"Now, why in the hell did you do that? We don't have anything to do with this shit!" Asher says. "I want credit for all my socks,"

"Since there are no socks left on the table, no one gets any points,"

"Oh, you're going to have to see me after the party is over," Aryan says to Joseph as he walks past him.

"I can see you now," he says, mushing Aryan's head, so Aryan punches him in his kidney, making Joseph buckle as he reaches for his side.

"Sit your old ass down, Joseph, before you get hurt."

"Please try it," Joseph says.

"Can we behave with some decorum, please? This is, afterall, Parker and Jaasiel's baby shower ,and I know y'all better get back over here and clean this mess up," Savvy says and we hurry to do what we are told. Not so much because she told us to, or the fact that we should, but once again, no one wants to anger Josh, and the quickest way to do that is to piss Savvy off.

"Okay, now it's the women's turn. The rules are the same they have sixty seconds to make as many matches as possible. Whoever gets the most correct matches wins!" Josh says as the women take their place at the table. "Ready, set, go!" he yells and they begin.

"At this point, all they have to do is get one match to win because you two dickheads gotta act like fucking toddlers," Jaasiel says to Joseph and Atlas.

"He started it," they say in unison, making us all shake our heads.

"I swear you two didn't mature past pre-school," Asher says.

"That's not fair!" Anson yells out, bringing our attention back to the women. Who are separating the socks by color and making pairs together.

"There's no rules against it," Josh tells them. "Times up!" he calls and the women have almost every sock in a pair. "Savvy wins this one with twenty-one pairs!" he yells out kissing Savvy.

"Figures, I mean she does have the most children," True says.

"Plus she's a grandmother," Carla adds in, and Savvy rolls her eyes at them both.

"The way you were going, you almost caught up too, Miss Hot-In-The-Pants," she says to Carla, who cocks her head to the side in contemplation before nodding her agreement.

"I mean, have you seen my husband," she asks with absolutely no remorse whatsoever.

"And the women take this round," he says, looking over to us like he is disappointed.

"Alright, guys, you're up." True calls out again. "These are dirty diapers, and you have to throw them in the garbage, aka the bucket over there. Whoever gets the most in, in sixty seconds, wins."

"Is there stuff in the diapers?"

"Yep, so be careful because you will be responsible for cleaning up your mess," she tells them with a little smirk on her face. "Ready, set, go!" she yells, and we begin throwing dirty diapers across the room into the buckets. Now this is a challenge we excel at. I pick up a diaper, and I feel Skai work her hand under my shirt and begin making circles on my chest and the diaper misses the bucket by a mile. I move her hand, quickly picking up another diaper, readying to throw it, and she plasters herself to my back, and this time, the diaper hits the wall. I look at my brothers, and they are all having similar problems. Joseph has completely given up on the game altogether and is in a heated lip lock with Joyce. "Times up!" True yells as she moves away from Atlas.

"Now that's a damn shame," Jaasiel says, laughing at us. Not one of us got a diaper in the bucket. I am glad the kids are off in another room watching a movie, cause some of the shit that was going on was R rated and moving into XXX.

"Once again, the men did not score. Time for the women," she says, sashaying away from Atlas. The women line up to play the game, Josh yells, "Ready. Set. Go!" We are on them before they can throw their first diaper, but much to our dismay, they still throw diapers. Skai is on the end opposite her mother so I know she cannot see what I am about to do to her daughter. Leaning over, I whisper, "Are your panties damp with my cum?" and her diaper goes clear across the room.

"Jabarri," she hisses, frantically, looking around to make sure no one heard me.

"I am going to have you dripping on the sheets all night," I tell her, pushing up against her. I watch her grip the edge of the table, and I know she's turned on and dripping our mixture in her panties. "If your panties weren't wet before, I know they are now," I tell her just as Josh calls, "Time! It looks like the women win this one, too."

"Wait how?" I ask, trying to figure out who could resist their husband.

"Savvy got three in her bucket."

"Turncoat," Atlas says when we sit down at our table.

"When she told me what she had in store for me later if I left her alone and let her shoot, it was a no brainer," he says unapologetically and truthfully once he put it that way I understood.

"Alright, the women have two, and the men have a big fat zero! Since there are only three games that means the women have won the baby shower game off! There is one final game for us all to play together so Momma B is going to take over," True says. A few minutes later, we all have a string tied around our waist with a pacifier hanging at the end.

"Alright, the objective is to swing the pacifier and catch it in your mouth. The first person to get the pacifier in their mouths, wins. This game is not timed so, ready, set, go!" she says and we all begin rocking our hips to make the pacifier swing. We look absolutely ridiculous, at one point, Aryan and Anson's string gets tangled, Joseph looks like he's bowing instead of swinging his hips. Josh and Asher got their pacifiers swinging pretty good but they keep missing their mouths. I focus on my pacifier and rock my hips, building up a nice swing before I lung at it and miss. I swear I look like a giant chicken. My string comes loose, so I take a quick few seconds to retie it and begin moving again. I swing the pacifier up, catching it in my mouth. I shoot both hands in the air in victory, spinning around showing everyone my win.

"I mean it makes sense since he just got off of the pacifier a few years ago," Atlas laments, making everyone else chuckle, including me. We end up sitting around talking, laughing, and eating until one by one we head off to bed, and for the first time I have the woman I have loved for years by my side. I take her hand and head towards our bedroom. "You better wake up. We have some unfinished business to attend to," I tell her when she yawns. "You can sleep on the plane," I suggest as I close and lock our bedroom door.

Skai

Ugh, it's been a few weeks since we came back from Florida, and I want to go back now! It was so peaceful and relaxing I didn't have to look over my shoulder or have an armed guard with me every minute of the day. I don't know how much longer I need to have all of this protection when literally nothing has happened. When I get home tonight, I am going to talk to Jabarri about stopping all of this. I check the time, and realize that I am running late picking up my dress. I will try it on, and if there is no issues I will take it home. Shepp, is really getting married! That was one reason he and Saint didn't come to the Keys with us. They were knee-deep in preparation. He and Isabella did not want a big wedding, just her parents, brother, sister and of course, her daughter. Now Shepp didn't have that luxury. He has me and Saint, my mom, and our dad and his wife, our other siblings from our dad, and then we have the Gideons, along with GrandPeter and GrandDoctor. or GD, that's what I call Lennox. I remember her reaction when I called her that, she was so happy. "I was wondering if I would ever get a nickname, too, but I wouldn't have asked or expected it. I know how much y'all loved Savvy's mom and miss her."

"True, but we love you, too, just like we love GrandPeter, and we love how much you love each other. So even though I had an amazing grandmother, you are an amazing GrandDoctor, and I wanted you to know that. I know she would have loved you, but is GD too masculine?"

"Nope, don't you dare try to change my name," she says immediately. "Besides, it fits perfectly next to Peter's GP," we hugged and she's been GD ever since.

That doesn't include the twins, the triplets, Dr. Mack, the General and Bree, Praise and Eli, yes, they are dating, and it is too cute. He is totally head over heels for her. Then there is T'Aundrea, Angie, and Malachi, our Aunt Bailey and Aunt Shell. Our mom's side of the family alone is about fifty people. So it's a hundred or less people type of small wedding. I step out of my office, and there is Emerson, "You're shift?" I ask. "Yes, but I need to pick up my dress, too, and I was looking forward to hanging out with you today," she says and I immediately feel guilty. The people guarding me are my family, and they love me and only want me safe and I am being a baby about it.

"Then let's make a day out of it," I tell her, sending a text to my boss letting her know I am working from home the rest of the day. "We'll grab our dresses, then grab lunch and perhaps do a little shopping."

"Sounds good to me," she says, sending a text, no doubt letting someone know we are on the move. The dresses fit perfectly and no alterations were needed, so we took them and put them in the back of the car as we headed for lunch. There's a new BBQ joint that I have heard good things about, so we head there and get shown to our seat. We take a few minutes to go over the menu, but I already know I want pulled pork, cowboy baked beans, mac and cheese with hush puppies and sweet tea. We give our order when the server comes back over, and Emerson is getting the same thing as me.

"How are things between you and Jabarri?"

"Wonderful," I say, blushing. "It's so nice not having to hide, having everything out in the open with our family and that they are okay with it and support us. Deep down, I was worried how they would feel, you know? I love DJ and all of his brothers, but there was always something different about Jabarri, but under those circumstances, I refused to even consider looking into it. Although, knowing what I know now, maybe if I had, I could have saved myself, Jabarri, and Alayna a lot of heartache."

"You can't do that to yourself. You did the best you could under your circumstances. In the end, things worked themselves out, not the way you anticipated, and maybe a lot hurtful, but in the end, it was what was best for you,"

"Yeah, I guess you are right." I contemplate her words, and I know I would have never given Jabarri a chance on my own. I had to be hurt, seek therapy, and heal before I was ready for his love. It hurt, a lot, but in the end, it pushed me right where I needed to be. "How are things between you and Liam?" And I see something I have never thought to see. Emerson blushes and turns shy. Well, that wasn't on my bingo card.

"It's more than I could have ever anticipated. He is everything. He was so much of what I didn't know I wanted or needed. And princess treatment is an understatement. He doesn't try to change me or dim my light. He isn't intimidated by me, my knowledge, or my skills. I love him so much. When he got shot at the baby shower, I saw everything that could have been flash before my eyes and disappear. When I realized he was okay, I knew then I would never leave his side."

"You're married!" I gasp.

"We're married," she confirms and proceeds to tell me everything. I am crying with her by the time she is done telling their story. "If you could keep it to yourself, I would really appreciate it. We want to tell everyone when the time is right."

"I mean, I'm going to tell Jabarri, but we will keep your secret,"

"That's fair, I don't keep anything from Liam either,"

"I mean, this might be a stupid question, but Eliza does know, right?"

"It's not a stupid question, and yes, she knows."

"I am so happy for you guys. I'm happy for all of us," I tell her just as the server brings our food. Liam is a gentle giant, he has taken care of Aunt Parker for years, and now he is Emerson's husband, and from the blush creeping across her face, he is taking amazing care of her. It's crazy to think of all the ripples in the water from one pebble being thrown in the water, my mom. Her running into DJ changed the trajectory of so many lives. Everything really does happen for a reason. We eat our food, talk about the wedding, the baby shower that they missed, and everything in between until it was time to head back home. We never even got to go shopping.

CHAPTER 20

*S*kai

The wedding was beautiful, and Isabella was a beautiful bride. Shepp gave her daughter a necklace when he gave Isabella her ring and had everyone in attendance in tears. Saint was his best man, and I was his best woman. Of course, our granddad officiated the wedding, and much to all our surprise, he brought his wife with him, and my mom actually talked to her. This world is definitely coming to an end. Once they said I do, we put the kids to bed with the grands and partied like it was 1999! I have never seen my brother happier, and just think he didn't even want to go to college. And not only did he go and finish, he excelled and took over GP's empire, with ease and panache. He has grown GP's brand, and GP has allowed him to create, and offshoot of his own under the Bennet umbrella, and it is doing well. He is a millionaire in his own right and he is only two years older than me. He used to come to me asking for money, but now I go to him. My mom and the other wives gift each other charm bracelets when they marry into the family but we chose personalized cuff bracelets. It was jewelry that even the guys can wear.

I look at my work desk and realize I have not really gotten anything done today at all. I have been reliving the wedding, and I am ready to really begin planning my wedding, too, and even in the midst of the uncertainty and drama I am going to begin planning it. My stomach's loud grumble lets me know I need to go get lunch. There is a spot all the way in the basement that makes the best tuna melts, and I am not leaving the campus so no need for a chaperone. I grab my keys, cell phone, ear buds, and wallet and head out. I jab the down button on the elevator and wait, but after waiting a long few moments and another stomach grumble, I decide to take the stairs. I take them two at a time, making light work of the flights until I get to the door that will lead me out to the floor. I am past the lunch hour, so it is pretty empty down here.

"Hey, Ms. Doris," I say to the lady behind the counter. Ms. Doris is retired and picked up the job to have something to do once all of her kids got married and moved away.

"Hi, baby, your usual?"

"Yes, ma'am," I say and grab a *Nehi Peach Soda* from the cooler as Ms. Dora puts together my sandwich. She makes short work of putting my sandwich together as we talk about life.

"Here you go, Skai," she says, handing me the large sub. "I swear I don't know where you put all this food. You're as skinny as a rail," she says the same thing every time I come down here to eat.

"Right here, Ms. Doris," I tell her, patting my stomach. I tap my debit card on the machine and head back to the stairwell. Maybe if I put my calories at a deficit by taking the stairs, it will make up for me getting ready to eat this entire sub and drink this whole soda. I take the steps two at a time. I get to the third floor and run into someone else on the stairs, she's tall, almost six feet. She puts me instantly on alert. I know this is a school, so people being in the stairwell is a common occurrence but she is like a cactus among roses. She just doesn't fit. But then again I think to myself she could be a new student or hell even a new staff member. We pass each other, and I continue to the fourth floor. I grab the knob but it won't turn. And then I feel it someone is coming up behind me.

"It would seem you are locked in here with me," the woman from earlier says with a think Spanish accent.

"Is that a fact?" I ask her.

"It is, but do not worry, I will make this quick."

"Oh, I am sure it will be quick because contrary to your earlier statement, I am not locked in here with you, you're locked in here with me," I tell her seconds before swinging the bag with my good ole sandwich in it and hitting her across her temple. I kick her kneecap, smiling in satisfaction at the loud crack and pop sound, and I know I've broken it. She drops down screaming, crying, and holding her leg. I grasp the soda, pull back and punch her in the temple before kicking her in her chest. When she falls back, I stomp her throat, crushing her windpipe and killing her instantly. I am breathing heavy when I am done. "Damn, that was my lunch," I say to myself when my stomach once again growls out her displeasure. I grab my phone, "Call Barbie," I tell it as I reach down and pull out the one segment that is still in the wrapper, and take a bite waiting for him to answer.

"Hey, baby," he says into the phone.

"We have a problem," I say without preamble.

This is a fresh hot mess. I think as I look at my family flip the hell out about the attempt on me today. Jabarri and all his brothers showed up and took care of the body, but now they really want to put me on restriction. My mom is holding me like she's scared that if she lets me go I will disappear.

"This is the worse time to not have the safety of the compound," Atlas says.

"Wasn't too secure when Nabeck came knocking," DJ says, reminding all of us why they are no longer living under one roof.

"Maybe, but the only reason we walked away from that is because we were there together, had they caught us one by one, I don't know if all of us would be here to talk about it right now," Joseph says, making us all nod in agreement.

"I called Doone. He's on his way. He said he was just getting ready to call us," Uncle Atlas says. It doesn't take long for Doone to get there.

"Atlas," he says as he shakes his hand. "So here's what I found out. Art is the new leader of Victor's old organization. He had a few people ahead of him but they either came up dead or missing.

It got to the point where no one was bold enough to challenge him. He is just as crazy and ruthless as Victor was. He even went as far as rebuilding Victor's house. Under his leadership, Art has expanded the organization to include cocaine, crack, meth, fentanyl, X and any other drug you can think of, and he has included weapons to what he sells. The only thing he doesn't sell is young girls and boys...yet. I think the woman that showed up was a scout. I am sure there will be more coming."

"So basically another Victor?" DJ surmises.

"It looks that way, yes."

"Doone?" Atlas inquires.

"It's just a feeling. I am going to keep digging," he tells us. "Watch your back. He's quite a handful, and if you need cleanup, just give me a call," he says, shaking Uncle Atlas' hand before leaving as fast as he came.

"Well, it looks like this time when we take the head of this organization out, we need to dismantle it as well. We are not looking over our shoulder for the rest of our lives," DJ says and I release a breath. This is manageable, I know they are going to rain hell down on this Art and then everything can go back to normal.

Jabarri

"Nöku Ahi?"

"Huh," She asks, her face glued to the screen like she hasn't seen this move a million times.

"Don't you think it's time for us to pick a date," I suggest, gaining all of her attention.

"You think so?"

"Yes, we know where the threat is coming from and we are working on shutting it down soon. Plus there hasn't been another attack on you and it's been a few weeks so yeah, let's get to planning."

"How about a year from now,"

"How about you try again,"

"Okay, well I don't want a big wedding, the same size as Shepp's wedding so I think we can get it done in a few months," she says, and it was music to my ears.

"Well, if we are going to do that, then let's put together an engagement party,"

"I think we can do it in a couple of weeks. I can ask Shepp about the hotel ballroom, and get invitations, it's only a few people coming from out of town so it shouldn't be a problem. I guess I have to invite my father and wherever he goes his wife has to tag along," she says rolling her eyes.

"Well, after the ass whooping your mother gave her the last time she was here, I'm sure she'll think twice before making any stupid ass comments,"

"I hope so because I am sure my mom won't mind beating her ass again. Okay, Shepp says give him the dates, and he will make it work," she tells me, tapping away on her phone responding to whatever her brother is saying to her.

"Let's say a month, the second Saturday, that should give the out of town family time to get here."

"Okay," she says, hopping up from the sofa where she was buried in my side, leaving me feeling bereft. A few minutes, she comes back with her laptop, and begins banging away at the keys, movie forgotten. We research invitations, choose some, and input the information once Shepp confirms the date. Skai told me that once he took over the hotel, he took one of the ballrooms off of the books reserving it for family events and only rents it out in extreme emergencies, along with a block of rooms, he also took the second highest floor to remodel all the rooms into suites for us too. So luckily for us there was no emergencies so the room was open. Invitations ordered, we contact the same party planning company we use for all of our events, and they were more than happy to accommodate us. I mean the huge tips we tend to leave and huge bills we rack up probably had something to do with that.

"I think I will call Mercy and see if she can design my engagement and wedding outfits. She did such an amazing job on Megan and Brooklyn's dresses, and I have to have one of her creations. Hopefully, she can squeeze me in, since she's blown up," Skai says once again texting I'm assuming Mercy. "Hot damn, we're in business. She says she has something she just made she thinks would be perfect for me but if not she will be more than happy to make me something. You better get your clothes together, sir,"

"Don't worry about me, my wardrobe game is tight,"

"Excuse me!"

"Do you want Jaasiel and Praise to cook?"

"Now you know I want Uncle Jaasiel and Praise to cook, but I also want them to just enjoy themselves, so I guess we'll have to deal with subpar food." She is practically pouting.

"I'll ask Jaasiel for some recommendations, and maybe we can get close to their level of food. You know how picky he is."

"Yes, true," Skai agrees, and we spend the rest of the evening planning our party and wedding. She is right, I have to get my clothes together.

"Baby, I know you are sending an invitation to your dad, but don't you think you should call and let him know before he just gets an invitation in the mail?"

"No," she says not lifting her eyes from the screen. While we are contacting people for the engagement party we are also booking them for the wedding, too.

"Nalani," I warn.

"Fine, and I guess I better call my granddad, too. I know he is going to talk trash about just being here,"

"I don't know why Pastor Errington doesn't just move here."

"Well, his wife lived in South Carolina, and as you know, my mom didn't care for her, but recently, my mom has made an effort to at least be cordial to her. So maybe when he comes up, we can try to convince him and his wife to move here."

"Why not? What's the worse that can happen?"

"Exactly,"

I still feel like I need to pinch myself. I am marrying Skai Errington, soon to be Gideon.

CHAPTER 21

Skai

Dammit! How am I late to my own party? I think, rushing around the room like a chicken with its head cut off. The outfit Mercy made is perfection, the beaded sleeveless pantsuit with detachable train. I channeled my inner Aunt Parker and went with all white with a few pops of yellow. My hair and makeup are done. Now all I have to do is get my ass in the car. I grab the rest of my things and stuff it in my purse and rush out of my bedroom. Ugh, I should've gone with Jabarri's suggestion of us going together, but I wanted to surprise him with my outfit. *Fuck it,* I think if I have forgotten something, oh well. Everyone is either en route to the hotel or already there, including my dad and granddad. *I swear to goodness if Jabarri texts me one more time!* I scream in my head. *Shit,* my flats! I grab them and head to the car. I open the Jeep door and throw my stuff in the passenger side. I put my foot on the bar, preparing to get in the car when I hear my phone ringing. I drop my foot back down and listen for the ringing. It's obviously not in the car, it sounds too far away. I start to pat myself down but stop when I realize there is no place on this outfit to stash my phone. *Dammit!* I threw it on my bed after Jabarri texted me for the twentieth time. It's a good thing this makeup is waterproof, it's hotter than doughnut grease at a fat man convention out here. I grab my key fob, rushing back in the house to grab my phone. I hit the remote start so the air can come on and hopefully cool down those hot-ass leather seats. Suddenly, I am thrown in the air landing hard on my side several feet down the hallway. *What! The! Hell!* I try to think around the ringing in my ears and pain in my side. I try to get up, but everything hurts. I drag myself to my room, pulling on the bedspread making shit clatter to the ground all around until, finally, my phone falls.

"Baby, you're late even for you."

"Jabarri," I gasp out before everything goes black.

Who is yelling? I think as I struggle to open my eyes. As I become more conscious, I realize no one is yelling. They are just talking but everything is in stereo for me.

"Can y'all please hush," I whisper out, and seconds later Jabarri is holding my hand.

"Skai, open your eyes, baby,"

"Okay," I say, but it takes so much effort that I am tired before I figure out how to do it.

"Please, Skai, I need to see your eyes." I hear him say, and I fight against the sleepiness trying to pull me back under and eventually crack my eyes to see Jabarri looking scared and downright furious.

"Hey, baby," he says, smiling at me.

"Water?" I ask, but before he can give me any much-needed water for my dry mouth, a nurse and doctor are in the room poking and prodding me. *So I'm in the hospital*, and it all comes rushing back to me. I was in the garage getting in the car, and went back inside to find my phone. I used the remote start, and then I was shot down the hall.

"What happened? How long have I been here?"

"Your car exploded, and just a few hours," Jabarri says.

"Jabarri, I was almost in the car. If you hadn't texted, making me throw my phone, I would have had it on me, and I would have been in the car. I would've been dead."

"You're okay, baby. They didn't get to you. By the time I got to you, the house was on fire but luckily, you closed your bedroom door, delaying the fire getting to you. This was too close, baby. We are going after them as soon as the doctor lets you go home.

"I am ready to go home now, I'm fine. Y'all aren't going without me,"

"I bet we are."

"No, you are not, Jabarbie!" I say, forgetting about the massive migraine and pain in my side.

"Let me tell your little ass something, You Are Not Going! I refuse to lose you. I will let you have anything else but not this. You will stay home. If you went and got hurt or worse I would be destroyed. I will happily crawl down into the depths of hell and make a deal with the Devil to eradicate every trace of them, all of their family, friends, exes, and anyone else they were associated with and I will dance in the fires of hell happily as long as it means you are safe. You cannot begin to comprehend how much I love you, Skai, so when I say you are not going, I mean that shit. I would rather you be mad at me alive, hell I would even accept you telling me you won't marry me if I don't let you go. As long as it means you are alive, safe, and whole. You are my heart not metaphorically either. You are the physical manifestation of my heart. I would simply die without you. So do us both a favor and not fight me on this."

"Am I interrupting?" Lennox says when she walks in to Skai and I having a stare off.

"No," she answers, turning to look at Lennox.

"They wanted to keep you for another twenty-four hours, but I have convinced them to send you home. It's good to know I still have some pull here," she says about her old hospital. "I am going to go back out there and get the accelerated version of the paperwork," she throws over her shoulder as she walks out. Personally I think it was to give Jabari and I a chance to finish our conversation.

"I'll stay home," I tell him. If I wasn't so frustrated at being left out of this fight I would've cried from his heartfelt words. "Where is my mom?"

"She walked out right before you woke up. She was talking to your dad,"

"Gotcha. I am sure he is trying to push all of her buttons."

"Get dressed," Lennox says when she comes back in my room.

"I ruined my outfit,"

"I got you something to wear," he says holding up a bag. He helps me get dressed, and I notice the bruise covering my whole right side. As soon as I am dressed in the graphic tee and leggings when my mom walks in.

"You're up. Lennox says you're able to come home."

"Where are we going to go?" I ask Jabarri, seeing as part of my house is either blown up or burned to high hell. And the house he was at the resort has been rented out since he was always at my house.

`"We are going to stay at the hotel,"

"But first, we are all going to the house to talk," my mom orders, and I groan partly because I am in pain, but I am not telling them that, and the other part is I do not want to hear what they have to say. "Then you and Jabarri can go rest, the talk shouldn't take too long," she says, and an hour later, we are all sitting in the beach house waiting.

"We are going to head to Texas, early in the morning and we are going to take Art and everyone else that is in there out. Once we do that, we are going to hunt everyone in that organization down and we are going to kill them all," DJ says.

"Sounds like my kind of party," Atlas says.

"Mine, too," True backs him up.

"Oh yeah, big surprise," Parker says, laughing because we all know those two always want the contact.

"We will go tonight. I am sick of the people closest to me getting hurt. So the sooner we can six-foot this Art person the sooner I can relax again."

"I'm down,"

"Me, too,"

"Hell, we can leave now,"

"Now who is that?" Aryan asks when the doorbell rings. ON the other side of the door are Doone and my dad.

151

"What are you doing here, Doone," Atlas asks him as they both walk in taking a seat.

"I was wrong. I knew I was missing something. There really wasn't a good angle of the man killed, but I took the video to a master 3-D sketch artist, and they completed the persons face, and it's Mark Hartman,"

"Why does that name sound so familiar?" Asher asks.

"Because he was in the news during the last election. He is the male version of *Olivia Pope*."

"Oh yeah, I remember, them saying he was missing, and they presumed him to be dead but have not been able to find his body," my mom says, "but how is he tied to Art?"

"Art's sister is married to the United States Secretary of Homeland Security. That's how he has been able to expand the business. From what I can glean, Art does the Secretaries dirty work, and the Secretary keeps him safe,"

"So that means what?"

"That means Art is untouchable. John Johnson will have the Gideons wiped out with a flick of the wrist. You can't kill your way out of this, and they will keep coming for not just Skai but all of you."

"Well fuck," I say, cussing in front of my mom.

Jabarri

Just when I thought there was light at the end of the tunnel, the bitch caves in. Not only do we have a psychopathic drug dealer after Skai, but he also has the Secretary of Homeland Security on his side. We might be fucked on this one.

"So, what do you suggest?" Savvy asks, coming over to wrap her arms around Skai. Everyone is here, both of Skai's brothers, her granddad and his wife, her dad and his wife, my mom and dad, and the regular crew.

"Witness protection,"

"Isn't ole boy over the witness protection program?"

"He is but I would handle it personally, off of the books. I have given quite a few people a new life. Like the girls you rescued from Victor's house, Atlas," Doone reminds Atlas. "But she wouldn't be able to contact anyone anymore. For intents and purposes Skai Errington would no longer exist," he says looking around the room.

"Hell no!" one of her brothers says, but I am too shocked to say anything.

"If someone has a better idea, I am all ears. You guys have never dealt with someone in the US as connected as these two. Johnson could say anything. He could fabricate allegations on Skai, have her arrested, and dropped in a black site. And while you are battling that, Art will be sending a steady stream of killers after her. She has to disappear, there is no other way." The more Doone talks, the more tears flow from both Skai and Savvy's eyes.

"I will already have all the paperwork I need for her,"

"Good, I'll need paperwork, too," I say. "Cause I am going, too."

"No! There has got to be another way!" Savvy screams. "I can't lose another child, I won't!"

"At least she will be alive," Doone tries to reason. "We need to move asap. Jabarri, I will have your paperwork ready for you by tomorrow."

"This is your fucking fault! If you weren't so busy and hell bent on being a bed wench to this white boy, our daughter wouldn't be in this mess!" William snaps. "Was whoring yourself out to this bitch worth it?"

Everything freezes and then speeds up, as Josh hits him so hard in the face that we all hear the bone snap. He unleashed a flurry of punches at William, who was caught so off guard that he didn't get a chance to prepare himself for the fight.

"I played with you before, but not this time! I got your bitch, mother fucker!" Josh yells his fists continuing to rain down on William in a savage onslaught. He catches him with an uppercut, forcing him to bite his lip with so much force it splits in two. William finally begins to put up a fight, but Josh kicked him in the chest sending him flying backward. It happened so fast none of us was prepared, by the time it clicked for us, we were in motion to pull Josh back as Skai cried and Savvy tried to comfort her daughter. By the time we got to Josh, William looked like he was been hit by a truck literally. Lennox rushed over to him to assess the damage and she began getting him fixed up.

"You can stay unless you need to go to the hospital, but if you stay, you better watch what the fuck you say. There is a lot of acreage you could get lost on."

"We'll be ready in the morning," I say when I sit back next to Skai. "We'll be together, and I will figure out a way to contact your mom, baby,"

"But we'll never see our family again. How do I do that?"

"You won't have to," my mom says. "I have something to tell you all."

CHAPTER 22

*J*abarri

We all take a seat, to hear what my mother has to tell us and how that will help us with protecting Skai. I know her and Savvy are desperate to keep their babies near them, but I will do anything to keep Skai safe including walking away from my family for her.

"What is this about, Mama?" Josh asks.

"Just take a seat," she says, looking at our dad who gives her a little head shake to encourage her. "I hope my sister will forgive me for this, but under the circumstances, I do not see another way. Atlas, Asher, Aryan, and Anson I have been keeping something from you. I was sworn to secrecy in order to protect you, but that is no longer necessary. Growing up, Berkley and I always looked out for each other, we were inseparable, and the same sense of family I instilled in each of you, was instilled in us. When I met Hemi and she met Alexander, we were so happy for each other, buying homes relatively close to each other so we could be there for each other and our families. I think when Victor's organization came for help expanding their drug empire, she knew it wouldn't end well. We had already talked and agreed that if anything should happen to one of us the other would take care of our children, but one day, when I was over having a girls day with her and our husbands took you boys out, she confided in me. Your grandfather, your father's father, Rory, ran from Ireland with your grandmother Saoirse (Sheer-Sha), the wife of his twin brother, Ronan," she drops that bomb and it leaves us all silent.

"Excuse me," Atlas says.

"You see, Rory saw Saoirse first, as a matter of fact, they fell in love. Their father, Rian, ran the biggest and deadliest crime family in Ireland. Ronan was the oldest brother by two minutes, and Rory was of course the baby, but it went deeper than that. Ronan's temperament was the mirror image of Rian's, mean, non empathetic, and just downright psychopathic. Rory, on the other hand, was like his mother, loving, kind, and generous, the complete opposite of everyone else in his family. Rory was considered a momma's boy and left to be with his mother since Ronan was more than happy to help his father run the organization. At the ripe old age of ten, he massacred an entire family with no remorse. One day, when Rory was about seventeen, he was sent to the store for his mother, and Saoirse was the cashier, she was beautiful, long curly red hair, big, kind green eyes, and a warm smile, needless to say, they were immediately taken with each other and before long, Rory was going to the store every day to see her. Now, where he messed up was when he brought her to the house to meet his mother. When he was leaving to take her home, Ronan walked in, took one look at Saoirse, and wanted her. It did not matter that his brother loved her or she loved him. Ronan went to Rian and Rian told Rory that since Ronan was the oldest brother it was his right to have any woman he wanted, including the woman he was in love with. He told him he would eventually find another woman. So when Ronan went to collect her, she had no choice but to go, since Ronan told her if she didn't, he would kill her entire family. He's reputation preceded him, everyone in Ireland knew how ruthless he was.

He married her as a way to keep her from his brother, but he became frustrated with the fact that no matter what he did she was still very much in love with his brother. It further aggravated him that no matter how many times he slept with her, she hadn't gotten pregnant. Thing went from bad to worse for her when the verbal abuse turned into physical abuse, and humiliation from the women he would flaunt in front of her and anyone else who was around. One month after he doubled his efforts to get her pregnant, and she fails to, he beat her so bad she was bedridden for a month. It was then that your grandfather Rory decided to take her and run with the permission and blessing of his mother.

One night, when Ronan was away with another woman, Rory killed the guard at the door, grabbed Saoirse and they ran. They first went to Scottland, but soon realized it wasn't far enough and hoped they would get lost in London's growing population. And it worked for a time, and they were able to be together, happily. It wasn't until his mother got word that Ronan was coming for them that he came up with a plan, they headed back to Scottland. They made sure to be seen and heard so it would be an easy trail to follow, once there they snuck back to Ireland where Rory's mother was waiting on him. She gave him enough money to secure passage to America and live a comfortable life. So while Ronan was in Scotland looking for them, they were on their way to America. One day, Rory bought a magazine, wrote a letter to his mother, and mailed it hoping it wouldn't get intercepted. A couple weeks later, he got his answer when a letter from his mother came inside of a magazine. They did this for several months. Sometimes, his mother would line the pages with more money to go along with her letter. The last letter he got his mother stated that Rian was getting more and more suspicious and Ronan had sworn to find him and kill him and Saoirse. She told him this would be her last letter and that she loved him very much she said he needn't worry about them finding out about the letters or where they are since she burned the letters after she read them. She also gave him the name and address of her most trusted confidant, Noreen, her attendant. Shortly after that letter, Noreen wrote him and told him Rian threw her off of a cliff, killing her. She also told him that Rian and Ronan vowed to avenge Ronan's honor by hunting them down and killing Rory, Saoirse, and any children they may have, and they would make sure every generation after would do the same until they were dead."

"Sonofabitch," Asher says.

"Your mother told me the story the same day she reminded me of our promise to take care of each other's kids if anything were to happen. She swore me to secrecy, she was worried about that family finding you and taking revenge like Rian had sworn to do decades prior. Shortly after coming to America, she became pregnant with Alexander. Come to find out, she was drinking a tea that kept her from getting pregnant. Once she stopped taking the tea, she got pregnant almost immediately and she had Alexander. Ronan got married again to a woman just as crazy as him and they had a son. Ronan convinced his son to take up the vendetta against Rory and Saoirse, and he did. Rownan was worse than his father but still couldn't find Rory, Saoirse, or Alexander. The letters kept coming, keeping Rory updated until Noreen died, and Rory and Saoirse died, married and happy. Also, Rownan got married and had three sons, he tried to get his sons to exact revenge, too. His oldest said he would, but once Rownan died his oldest son, Riagan, declared the blood feud was over. In his words *Fuair an cac sin bás le m'athair,* or that shit died with my dad.

You see, he was able to do what his father and grandfather before him could not, he found me. Imagine my shock when I answered my phone, and he was on the other end. He told me he had found me years ago but waited until his father died before reaching out. He swore he wanted nothing to do with the revenge plot. We talked for a long while and have continued to talk to each other at least once a week,"

"Ma, this is amazing to hear, but what does this have to do with the little menace over there?" Atlas asks.

"Watch it, Uncle Atlas!" Skai says.

"In the years since Rory left, the Brennan's empire has grown to cover the entire country of Ireland, they run the whole thing. Riagán and his two brothers Riacán and Rioghán control the entire country, nothing happens there without their say so or approval," my mom says.

"Okay so you want to send Skai and Jabarri to Ireland?" Josh asks.

"Yes."

"We have cousins?" Anson says in awe.

"Yes, you do."

"Aren't we your cousins?" Joseph asks.

"No, you're our brothers," Atlas says emphatically.

"Okay, but we don't even know if they will help and are you sure we can trust them? I would hate to have to fight Homeland Security, a drug cartel here, and a mob family in Ireland, too," Josh says to my mom as my dad gets up and walks away.

"Joshua, I trust them. And do you have a better idea?" she asks. Everyone looks around but no one is saying anything. "At least we can still see them, talk to them but if we do what Doone suggests they will forever be lost to us."

"That is unacceptable," Savvy says, still clutching Skai.

"I agree," my mom says.

"Fine mama, call them and let's see if Riagán, Riacán and Rioghán will be willing to help," Josh says, looking at me, Skai, and finally his wife, knowing he doesn't really have any other choice.

A noise from the doorway grabs our attention, and there stand three large red-headed menacing-looking men. They exude power and craziness in equal measure, and they look like they could be Atlas, Asher, Anson and Aryan's brothers they are clearly related. "We prefer to be called Lawless, Fury, and Savage, and we are more than willing to help, cousin," Lawless says.

To Be Continued…

Part 2 Coming Soon

ABOUT THE AUTHOR

J. Nell, a self-proclaimed accidental author, has found her voice in crafting tales of later-in-life interracial romance, where professional men and bold black women take center stage. Born and raised in the lively city of Rochester, situated in the fast-paced state of New York, J. Nell's storytelling is imbued with the dynamic energy of her upbringing.

For J. Nell, faith and family reign supreme, serving as the cornerstone of her life. When she's not surrounded by loved ones, she seamlessly weaves the demands of one or both of her full-time jobs into her daily routine, showcasing a remarkable work ethic and dedication to her professional pursuits.

In the moments of respite, J. Nell delves into her passions with gusto. A voracious reader, she explores the realms of literature, particularly delving into the complexities of later-in-life interracial romance. Beyond the pages, she unleashes her creativity in the kitchen, reveling in the art of cooking. Her love for exploration knows no bounds, as she traverses the globe, absorbing the diversity of cultures and landscapes.

Music and singing form the soundtrack to J. Nell's life, and she embraces her sports fanaticism with pride, especially when it comes to her beloved Denver Broncos. Sunday afternoons find her immersed in the exhilaration of football, feeding her addiction and cheering on her favorite team.

J. Nell's accidental journey into the world of literature reflects the richness of her multifaceted identity. A devoted advocate of later-in-life interracial romance, a culinary enthusiast, a globetrotter, a music lover, and an unapologetic football fan, she invites readers into a world where love transcends boundaries and life is a vibrant tapestry of experiences.

ALSO BY J. NELL

The Gideon Brothers & Friends

The Holiday Bad Boys

Club Desire Series

Mahogany's Heart

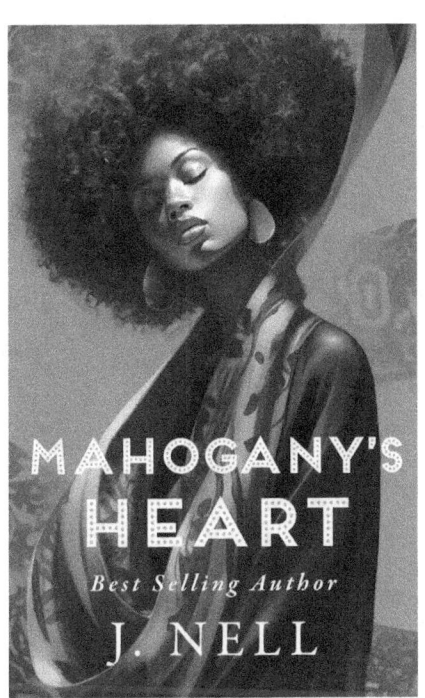

MAHOGANY'S HEART

Best Selling Author

J. NELL